# Contempt Of Court

Anne Sweeney Holliday

PublishAmerica

Baltimore

First printing

ISBN: 1-59286-923-8
PUBLISHED BY PUBLISHAMERICA, LLLP
www.publishamerica.com
Baltimore

Printed in the United States of America

# Chapter One

I can't help but smile when I walk into the courtroom and see her sitting there. I'm not surprised to see her. In fact, I expected her to be there. But seeing her today makes me smile.

Maybe it's because I need someone on my side today.

I don't know if she does it on purpose, but she always seems to find a way to make me look good. I could be having the worst day - loosing all my arguments, not connecting with the jury, pissing off the judge - and she'd still find a way to make Joe Manzarelli look as if he's the most brilliant lawyer in Brafferd County, Pennsylvania.

I'm no slouch, but I'd hardly say I'm brilliant, especially over the last few years.

Of course I'm not complaining about the way she writes about me. It just makes me wonder.

I also wonder why she always sits on the defense side of the courtroom. The other reporters sit on the prosecution side, with the good guys. But not her. She ... Damn! What is her name? I can never remember. Dina. Nina. Tina. No. No. No.

I should remember. We see each other at the courthouse at least once a week, more if I have a high profile trial. I'm the city's lawyer, so I see her when she covers the weekly city council meetings. She's always calling me about some city issue or ordinance or citizen complaint.

What is it that she says when she calls? If only I could remember …

But I'm digressing. I'm sure my client would be less than thrilled if he knew that on the day his murder trial is starting I'm thinking about a woman. I'm a bit confused by it myself. I haven't really thought about any woman since the divorce. I can't figure out why I can't get this woman out of my head today.

It couldn't be that wavy auburn hair falling softly over her shoulders. It couldn't be those emerald green eyes that sparkle when she gives me that demure smile. No, it couldn't be any of those things.

I wish I could get my hands on a newspaper so I could see her byline. (Katrina? No. Zina? Surely not.) But the judge ordered that no newspapers be brought into the courtroom. If I can put away this obsession at least until the first recess, I can grab a newspaper and put this out of my head.

I better find some way to get it out of my head earlier. Bill Valentine, the district attorney whose sole purpose in life is making my life a living hell, just entered the courtroom. The judge should be along shortly, seeing as how that's how it usually goes. Finish their old man gossip over a cup of coffee. Bill pops a breath mint into his mouth and comes the courtroom. The judge pops a mint, puts on his robe, then he enters. Been that way for as long as I can remember.

I use the time waiting for the judge to reassure my client that everything will be fine. No need to worry.

I wish I believed that.

I know he's innocent. Anyone with half a brain knows he's innocent - or will know after they hear the evidence. But convincing a jury of that is another story. The hardest part will be convincing them that old Bill Valentine didn't do his homework this time.

If I can't remember the last time he lost a case, I'm sure the jury can't. Of course juries aren't supposed to think about things like that, but they're human. We know they do. So it's my job to prove to them Bill Valentine is human. He makes mistakes. He made a mistake by bringing my client to trial, especially on murder charges.

I watch the jury as Valentine drones on about how the county is taking a tougher stance on drunk driving. That's why Michael Logan is charged with murder. He runs through all the reasons he'll be able to prove Michael Logan murdered Jessica and Philip Owens and their six-year-old daughter during that snowy Christmas Eve night on that winding piece of country road.

He's wrong. Now it's my turn to tell the jury why. I stand up, look at what's-her-name the reporter because I need to see a friendly face, nod to the judge, then slowly walk toward the jury box.

"Ladies and gentleman," I start, flashing my best you-can-trust-me smile, "Mr. Valentine just told you a sad, tragic story. What could be more tragic than a family being killed on their way to Grandma's house on Christmas Eve? Not many things, right?

"But there is one thing: Convicting an innocent man of killing that family. Michael Logan did not kill the Owens family. He wasn't driving the car that hit theirs and sent it sailing across the road and into the ditch. …"

By the time I finished my opening argument I think I had some of the jury members convinced I had a case.

I think I have what's-her-name the reporter convinced. At least that's what I think it meant when I saw her smiling as she tapped the keys on her laptop.

I've failed to mention so far that Bill Valentine is not only the district attorney. He's the king of sidebar conferences. Why he and the judge can't work these things out during their morning coffee, I'll never know. But, here we go up to the bench. It seems the state's first witness - a state police trooper - hasn't arrived yet because of a family emergency and Valentine would like the judge to call a recess until he arrives. After Valentine's request, there's a little talk about what bad shape the golf course at the country club is in. Then, we go sit down again before the judge calls the recess.

Although I tell him I have some business to take care of, my client decides he'd like to stay in the courtroom during the recess. Can't say as I blame him. Even if he can't talk to anyone but the guards and people who work in the courtroom, it's better to be there with people than in the holding area alone.

Now, I'm on a mission. I have to find a newspaper. What the hell is her name?

I can't tell you how frustrating it is to go to office after office looking for a newspaper only to hear they don't read the paper or they lent it to someone else or they threw it away already and it's covered with coffee grounds. My next stop is the court records office.

I see a newspaper sitting on a desk in corner. But I also see what's-her-name the reporter standing near the bank of computers for public use across the room. But she's not looking at a computer. She's looking at one of the record books that was used before everything was computerized.

I can't help but wonder what she's looking for. Why would she need anything that old?

I'll have to add that to the list of things I'm wondering about because one of the clerks just told me the witness has arrived and it's time to get back to the courtroom. Someone must have told what's-her-name, too, because she's walking toward the door. And me.

"Hi Joe," she says, with that smile that … Well, I can't explain exactly what it does to me. But it does something.

"Morning," I say as cheerfully as I can, hoping my tone will keep her from realizing I didn't use her name.

"You still don't remember," she says, shaking her head, but still smiling.

"Remember what?" I ask.

"My name."

"Oh c'mon. What makes you say that?"

"You never remember," she says, still smiling. "That could give a girl a complex, you know."

Before I can defend myself. Actually, I can't defend myself. But before I can make some witty comment that would make her forget I forgot her name, she's out the door and on her way to the courtroom.

If only I could remember that cute thing she says when she calls me. It always makes me smile. Now what is it? And what the hell is her name?

One of the clerks asks me if I want something. Probably because I have, as my daughter would say, a "duh me" look on my face. I tell the clerk I came in looking for a copy of the newspaper. She tells another clerk to grab that copy of *The Century* and hand it to me.

*The Century*. That's it. Trial of the century. Fight of the century. Gina of *The Century*.

Gina. Gina Hamilton.

I can hear her saying it now. Hi Joe. It's Gina of The Century. I need to know …

Now that that's out of the way maybe I can concentrate on clearing my client of murder charges. But I still can't help but wonder what Gina was looking for.

# Chapter Two

She did it again. Gina of *The Century* made me look good. Not that it was a hard job. I was good yesterday, but she made me look better than I was.

I wonder how much better she'll make me look when she finds out I remembered her name. I would have liked to let her know yesterday, but I didn't get a chance. Of course I could have walked right up to her in the courtroom and said "Hi Gina." But it didn't seem like the right time or place.

Maybe today. But first I should get dressed. I like this leisurely morning pace and I know I'll miss it when Kathryn gets here next week. But, as much as I like taking my time in the morning, I wouldn't trade Kathryn being here for anything in the world.

Kathryn's mother, my ex, is going on yet another vacation and, yet again, leaving our eight-year-old with me. I thought I'd have a hard time juggling work and Kathryn, but it's not nearly as difficult as I thought it would be. I think I do a damn good job of it. I hope the judge thinks so during the next custody hearing. How could he not? I'm here. Kathryn's mother - I suppose it wouldn't kill me to call her Vanessa - is off gallivanting in Aruba, Bermuda or - where is it this time? -- Cancun. What kind of parent is she anyway?

I shouldn't have gotten myself started on Vanessa. Always puts me in a bad mood, and I can't afford to be in a bad mood today. I have crucial evidence to present that could make or break the case. Actually, the evidence speaks for itself. The crucial part is convincing the jury that the district attorney's office ignored or overlooked it - and didn't care.

A shower, getting dressed and the 20-minute drive to the courthouse didn't erase my bad mood. Vanessa has a way of doing that to me. But the instant I walked into the courtroom and saw Gina of *The Century* I smiled.

Her laptop is booted up and ready to go but sitting next to her on the bench, but she's intently studying whatever is written in her notebook. She is so involved, in fact, that when I say good morning I startle her and she jumps a little.

"Sorry," I say, still not using her name and, for the life of me, I don't know why. "I didn't mean to scare you."

"No problem," she says, quickly closing her notebook and stuffing it in her purse. "I just, umm, got lost for minute."

"Lost?"

"Sometimes I get really involved in what I'm doing and I forget where I am. Doesn't that ever happen to you?"

"Yes, I guess it does." Awkward pause. "Oh, I wanted to thank you."

"Thank me? For what?"

"Today's article."

"No need to thank me," she says, smiling. "I write 'em like I see 'em."

"We'll you just keep seeing things the way you are. ... And don't get lost anymore today, okay?"

"Okay," she says, laughing. "I promise."

Gina was ready. I was ready. But I didn't get a chance to be brilliant. She didn't get a chance to write about my brilliance.

Court had barely been in session for 10 minutes when a bailiff came in with a note for the judge. He called Valentine and me to the bench and explained the situation. The judge sentenced a three-time drug offender to a halfway house rehab center instead of jail because he comes from a "good family." It seems that no matter how good your family is, when you want to get out of a halfway house, the most sensible thing to do is grab a butcher knife from the kitchen and threaten to slit a counselor's throat unless you can talk to the judge.

The judge, who has a reputation for being too easy on drug offenders, and looking out for people from "good families," postpones today's court session to talk to this person. I wonder if it has anything to do with the fact that this person's father is on the local college's advisory board, as is the judge.

As we walk away from the bench, Valentine looks at me, shakes his head and says "Drugs."

"Excuse me?" I say.

"Drugs," Valentine says. "I think you know what I'm talking about."

If we weren't in a courtroom I swear I could have strangled him to death and not given it a second thought. He never misses an opportunity to remind me about my past. Not that I was a heavy drug user - I'll admit I smoked a little pot on occasion. It was the '70s - but I was associated with people who were, and it wasn't always pretty. In fact, it was so ugly that I'm sure some people who knew me then would never have believed I'd end up defending criminals instead of being one.

I feel my mood deteriorating again and turn to look at Gina hoping her smile will get me out of this funk. But it seems that while I was getting all of my stuff together, she was doing the same and snuck out of the courtroom without even saying goodbye.

Maybe an early lunch or a snack would help, I think, so I head on over to the Courtyard Café across the street from the courthouse. I get my favorite table in the corner by the front window, order a cup of coffee and a piece of cherry pie a la mode and think. Brood is more accurate.

But then I hear a light tap on the window, look up at see that smile. Why didn't I ever notice before that Gina has this effect on me? If I'd realized it, I might have worked a little harder at remembering her name.

Gina waves then continues on her way, quickly walking back to the courthouse, occasionally sipping from a bottle of Diet Coke. As I watch her I keep wondering why I didn't notice her before. Actually, that's an easy question. I'm pretty dumb when it comes to women. Vanessa would be enough evidence to back that up.

I gulp down the last of my coffee, leave a tip on the table, pay my bill then head back to the courthouse. I do have other cases to think about and, as long as I'm here, I might as well get some work done.

Okay. Yes, I'm hoping to run into Gina.

And there she is standing near the bank of computers in the court records office again diligently taking notes while paging through an old records book. I watch her for about 10 minutes. Then someone else comes into the office, lets the door slam and makes her jump. She turns around, sees me, smiles nervously for some reason then slams the book shut and shoves it onto a shelf. She stuffs her notebook into her purse, then walks toward me.

"Hi Joe," she says, then adds with a wink and a smile, "Don't even bother. I've learned to accept the fact you'll never remember my name."

"Ah, but you're wrong Gina. Gina Hamilton. Gina of The Century."

"I don't know how to feel about that," she says, widening her eyes with mock shock.

"Keep 'em guessing," I say. "That's my motto."

"You have a motto?"

"No. Not really. But it sounded good."

She laughs. "Yes, it did. … I'd really like to stay and chat about more of your mottoes, but I should get back to work."

"Isn't that what you're doing now?"

"Yes," she says, starting to fidget, "but I still have to write a story about today's court proceedings … or lack thereof."

After we say our good-byes, I decide I need to know what old court records Gina has been so intent on. I ask one of the clerks and, after discovering what she's been looking at, my knees get a little weak. I have a bad feeling about this. I get a bad feeling anytime the Danny Dwyer murder case comes up.

I wish I knew why Gina was digging it up after almost 30 years.

# Chapter Three

I knew I'd have nightmares. I always do when I have any kind of extended thoughts about Danny Dwyer. Extended thoughts is an understatement of what was racing around my brain most of yesterday and last night.

No matter what I did, I couldn't get him out of my mind. I couldn't get Gina, and why she's digging up information about Danny Dwyer, out of my mind either. Surely if there was new information I would have heard about it. Even if no one directly involved in the investigation - if there still is an investigation after 30 years - told me about it, I would have heard it through the grapevine.

I'm sure Bill Valentine would take great pleasure in letting me know Danny Dwyer's unsolved murder was heading back into the spotlight. Just the appearance of impropriety on my part would make him the happiest man in the county. I don't know why he has it out for me, but he does. I'm sure of it. I can feel it. I have a feeling it has something to do with Danny Dwyer, but I can't figure that out either.

Danny was my best friend and, yes, he was heavily into drugs. But I tried stopping him. I tried stopping him the day he died - the day he was murdered. Valentine knows that. So why does he take every opportunity to rub drug offenders in my face. Hell, he knows I won't even represent drug offenders or drunk drivers.

I suppose it's another one of those unsolved mysteries. Maybe he doesn't like me and it's as simple as that. That's fine because I don't particularly care for him either. Call it karma. Call it intuition. Call it whatever you want. I just have a bad feeling about the guy.

My dislike for him should work to my advantage during closing arguments today. I'm sure the jury will feel my contempt for Valentine when I remind them that his office totally ignored the fact that there were three, not two, sets of tire tracks at the accident scene. I'm sure the jury will feel my utter disgust at the fact that Valentine's office failed to note the paint chips on the victims' car weren't even the same color as my client's vehicle, not to mention that the damage to the vehicles wasn't even consistent with Logan's vehicle hitting the Owens vehicle. I'm sure they'll be as appalled as I am when I remind them that police at the scene didn't even think to do blood alcohol or field sobriety tests because they didn't believe Logan was drunk.

Valentine blew this one. He probably thought a court-appointed defense attorney wouldn't put enough time and effort into this case to find the mistakes.

He underestimated me, and one of the great thrills of my life will be handing him his first lost case as district attorney. He should have let one of his flunkies handle this one, the way he does with all the cases he knows his office won't win.

Well, all my rambling thoughts got me to the courthouse before I knew it. It always freaks me out when I get to my destination but I forget the drive from point A to point B. But the important thing is I made it safely and I'm ready to kick ass - some Bill Valentine ass.

"Good morning counselor," Gina says as I set my notebooks and folders (I was never one for briefcases) at the defense table.

"Good morning Gina of *The Century*. Your nose isn't buried in a notebook this morning. That's different."

"I thought I should concentrate on this case today," she says.

"Oh. I thought you forgot it or lost it," I say, going on a fishing expedition, hoping she'll tell me what's in that notebook.

"Nope," she says, not taking the bait.

"Well, that's good I guess."

Another awkward pause. At least it's awkward for me. I don't think I'm imagining it.

I know I'm not imagining Gina standing up, standing on her toes and leaning toward me.

"Good luck," she whispers in my ear.

"Why are you whispering?" I whisper back.

"Can't play favorites," she whispers. "Objective reporter. Remember?"

We smile at each other then take our seats just before Bill Valentine enters the courtroom.

**\*\*\*\*\*\*\*\*\*\***

"Congratulations," Gina says as the judge leaves the courtroom. "You were great."

"I'm glad you think so," I say. "But I'm even more glad the jury thought so."

"Sure didn't take them long to reach a verdict, did it?"

"No," I say. "It surprised me that it was so quick."

"Me too. Uh. Well, I guess I should go back and write my story."

"I have a proposition for you Gina of *The Century*. Since we finished here much earlier than expected, why don't you take a little extra time and have lunch with me. You do have to eat after all, right?"

"I guess I do," she says. I swear she's blushing.

At the Courtyard Café we both order iced tea and decide to go to the salad bar. We talk a little about the case and I wonder if she's thinking the same thing that I am: How do we make the transition from work talk to personal talk?

Thank God she takes the plunge first and makes an almost seamless transition. Smart lady.

"Now that the trial's over," she starts, "do have any interesting plans or are there more trials in your near future?"

"No more big trials for a while - at least not anything you'd be interested in," I say. "So my immediate plans are to spend as much time as possible with a pretty young blonde."

"Oh really?" she asks, raising an eyebrow.

"Yeah," I say, satisfied with her reaction. "My daughter Kathryn will be spending a couple weeks with me while her mother lives it up in Cancun."

"That'll be nice," she says. "Do you get to spend a lot of time with your daughter?"

"Not as much as I'd like. Never as much as I'd like. But I'm hoping the next custody hearing will change that."

"Are you trying to get full custody?"

"You bet I am. My ex is the poster child for unfit mothers."

"Uh, a little bitter are we?"

"More than a little. I'll admit it. Since the divorce Vanessa's lifestyle has gotten even more out of control than it was during our so-called marriage. I don't want Kat subjected to that any longer. She's been through enough."

"Can I ask you something kind of personal?"

"Sure."

"Okay. You're a successful lawyer. You're smart, funny and, well, you're very attractive. How could Vanessa let you get away? I mean, what happened?"

"Simple. She couldn't keep her hormones in control," I say, trying to keep a proper amount of anger toward Vanessa in my voice instead of the excitement that I feel from Gina's compliments. "I forgave her the first time. I even agreed with her that it was partially my fault that she turned to someone else. I forgave her the second time because I didn't want to disrupt Kat's life. But the third time? No way. I couldn't live like that anymore."

"I don't blame you," she says. "So how is your daughter handling it?"

"She's great," I say. I'm sure I'm beaming the way I always do when I talk about Kathryn. "I know she gets upset sometimes about her mother's lifestyle but she's learned to accept it. That must be hard for an eight-year-old but she seems to be handling it quite well. And Vanessa will have to deal with the consequences when Kat gets older."

"Seems as if nothing's affected her swimming," Gina says.

"You're right," I say, surprised that she would bring up swimming. "My little girl is Olympics-bound. If determination is enough to get her there, she'll do it for sure."

"I've seen her in action," Gina says. "She's very talented."

"You've seen her?"

"Yeah. At the last swim meet at the college. I'd heard the sports department sing her praises and I wanted to see what all the fuss was about. Now I know. She's something else."

"Yes. Yes, she is," I say, beaming again. "But enough about me and Kat. Tell me a little about you."

"There's not much to tell. I work. I go home. I play online for a couple hours. I sleep. Repeat five times. That's my week."

"What about weekends?" I ask.

"I rent movies, play online a little longer, catch up on things I couldn't do during the week. I'm tellin' ya. Boring."

"So, what's a pretty girl like you doing leading such a boring life?" I say, surprised that I told her I think she's pretty.

"I ask myself that question a lot," she says, laughing. God, I love her laugh. "But I'm used to it and, well, I guess I'm comfortable with it."

"Comfortable but not happy?"

"I didn't say that."

"So you are happy?"

"I didn't say that either. I guess I'm kind of confused about that. And," she says, looking at her watch, "I'm kind of getting nervous about not getting back to the newsroom. I really should go write my story."

"Avoiding personal questions, I see."

"No. Well, not really. I, well … I just want to get this story done."

"Okay," I say. "Then maybe we can do this again sometime?"

"I'd like that," she says, standing up from the table. "So, I'll see you Tuesday?"

"Tuesday?"

"City council meeting."

"Oh yeah. Council. I'll see you Tuesday."

I watch her walk out the door and to her car parked across the street wondering if "see you Tuesday" was just a polite blow-off line. She said she wants to do this again sometime, but obviously she doesn't see it happening in the four days between now and Tuesday.

So much about her is a mystery - just like her interest in the Danny Dwyer case. I hadn't thought about that for hours.

# Chapter Four

I hear a chirpy, cheery "Goooooood moooor-niiiiiiing!" at about the same time I notice the bed bouncing. Or more accurately, Kathryn bouncing on the bed attempting to wake me up. I grab her, pull her down and hug her tightly.

"What are you doing up so early?" I mange to ask, still partially asleep I think.

"It's not early," she says, hugging me back. "It's 7. Normal time. But you didn't sleep well. That's why you think it's early."

"Well."

"Well what?"

"I didn't sleep well."

"That's what I said."

"Oh Kitty Kat," I sigh. "Let's get this show on the road."

I open my eyes to find out she's already dressed, so I'm the one holding up the show. I pick her up and put her on the floor, then get out of bed. She follows me to the bathroom.

"Daddy," she starts while doing a balance beam routine on the edge of the bathtub as I brush my teeth, "What were you dreaming about?"

"I don't remember," I lie, recalling yet another Danny Dwyer nightmare.

"I don't beee-leeeeeive you," she says.

"I don't caaaaa-aaaaare," I tease.

She laughs. I start shaving.

"Daddy," she says. "You should do something about that gray hair."

"What?" I ask, not quite sure if I should laugh or feel insulted that she noticed.

"It's not too bad yet," she says, "but you should do something about it before it gets yucky. Mom says that on some men gray hair is distin …. Um, distingis …. Um …."

"Distinguished?" I offer.

"Yeah. That's it. Mom says it can be dis-tin-guished, but it just makes you look old."

"Uh huh," I say, pretending I'm concentrating on shaving. "What else does Mom say?"

"She says you have the sexiest blue eyes she's ever seen."

"She told you that?" I say, putting down my razor and turning around to look at my eight-year-old.

"Not exactly," Kathryn says. "I kind of overheard her telling someone else."

"Eavesdropping, eh?"

"Yes," she says, her shoulders slumping.

"I'm not angry Kitty Kat," I say, hugging her. "I'm just glad you and your mother aren't discussing sexy blue eyes. I don't want you thinking about anyone's sexy blue eyes for at least another 10 years."

"Oh Daddy," Kathryn says, giggling. "Daddy?"

"Yes?"

"Does that lady at the newspaper think you have sexy blue eyes?"

"I don't know," I say, hoping that she does. "Why do you ask?"

"Just wondering."

"Wrong answer," I say, tickling her belly. "Why did you ask?"

"Well, you've been talking about her a lot and you went to lunch with her three times last week."

"We're friends," I say. "That's it."

"Okay. I was just wondering."

"I'll make you a promise, Kitty Kat. If I ever decide to start dating again you'll be the first to know. Deal?"

"Deal," she says. "Daddy?"

"Yes?"

"If Mom doesn't call tonight can we call her?"

"Of course we can," I say, hugging her tight.

Vanessa promised to call from Cancun every night but, aside from the 10-minute call to let us know she arrived safely, she hasn't called in four days.

And I'm the unfit parent?

\*\*\*\*\*\*\*\*\*\*\*

After dropping Kathryn off at school, I head to the office and tell my secretary Barbara I'm not accepting any calls except from Kathryn. I'm obsessed with Danny Dwyer and I need to look through the files I've tried to keep out of my mind for more than 20 years.

Files. I guess you could classify them as files. They're actually a cluster of newspaper clippings and a few notes I took just in case I needed to remember what I was thinking back then.

Or if anything ever came back to haunt me.

Call it a premonition. Call it paranoia. Call it too much experience in small-town living. But I had a feeling somehow, some way, someday the Danny Dwyer case would be a major part of my life again. The most disturbing thing right now is not knowing why - if, in fact she is - Gina is trying to open it up again.

Maybe that's paranoia as well. Maybe she's simply curious about it. Who knows? I almost don't want to know. I just want it to go away.

I don't know what an anxiety attack feels like, but I imagine what I'm feeling right now while digging out the file is pretty close. I feel all clammy. I'm a bit light-headed and dizzy. My heart feels as if it's beating at ten times its normal rate and could pound its way out of my chest at any second.

If just the anticipation of looking at the file is this bad, what am I going to feel when I start looking at everything and memories start coming back and everything becomes fresher and clearer in my mind. It'll probably be something like the nightmares, I'm sure.

When I think about it, I remember that the last six months of Danny Dwyer's life were a nightmare - to me anyway. It was probably more of a blur to Danny. When he started the downward spiral he fell faster than I could have imagined. I hated what the drugs and his

ANNE HOLLIDAY

so-called friends did to him, but I didn't see a way to stop him. In some ways I could see how death would be a relief to him. The only way out.

I stare at the first newspaper clipping in the file. I'm almost mesmerized by Danny's high school graduation picture that was used with the story. It didn't look anything like Danny the way he was when he died. Amazing what two years of hard living can do. The headline on the story reads "Son of prominent businessman dead." Then, underneath, a smaller headline reads "Police say drugs found at scene but foul play not suspected."

Foul play not suspected. To this day I don't understand that. I don't know if I ever will.

Danny died of a gunshot wound to the back of his head. Execution style. The police chief said it was suicide. The coroner agreed. Case closed.

Danny was a lot of things, but a contortionist wasn't one of them. It took an 18-month fight by Danny's father, David Dwyer, to get the case reopened. Twenty years later it's still open and, as far as I know, there's nothing to make anyone believe it will ever be closed.

Yet another of Brafferd County's unsolved murders.

# Chapter Five

As if my life needs more turmoil, I'm confused about my feelings for Gina. I order another glass of red wine while waiting for her to arrive for our lunch date. I can't tell if I'm honestly attracted to her, or if I'm simply obsessed with her interest in the Danny Dwyer case.

I've always found her attractive and I'll admit that even while I was still married I thought Gina was cute and charming. I found myself looking forward to her phone calls. Okay. I'll admit this, too. I even fabricated reasons to call her at work because I always felt so good after our conversations. I've always been pleased that she paints such flattering picture of me in her stories and I'd always hoped that it was because she had a thing for me. Even happily married guys need to know other women find them attractive.

But now I'm not sure if I want to spend time with her because I genuinely like her, or if it's a lame attempt to pump her for information. Maybe it's a little of both.

"Sorry I'm late," she says, sitting across the table from me. I didn't even notice her walk in. "I lost track of time."

"Seems you're always losing something," I say.

"No kidding," she says, dropping her car keys into her purse. I notice a notebook sticking up and wonder if it's the one containing the Danny Dwyer notes. "I'm so scatterbrained sometimes. I swear I'd lose my head if … No wait. I promised myself I was going to cut down on my use of cliches."

"You make promises like that to yourself?"

"Yeah," she says, hanging her head. "It's a word-geek thing. Sometimes I promise myself I'm going to learn a new word everyday. Sometimes I promise myself that I have to find some way to fit a certain word into a story. … Oh, it goes on and on. I won't bore you with it. It's strange."

"It's cute," I say.

"Really?" Gina asks, perking up a bit. "You think so?"

"Sure do."

"Thanks," she says, blushing.

"Now let's get back to you getting lost again."

"Oh. Well," she starts. She seems a little nervous. "I was at the courthouse doing research and just forgot to check the time. That's all."

"Must be some pretty interesting research."

"It is, actually."

"Care to elaborate?"

"Well," she starts. Now I know she's nervous because she's twirling her hair around her finger the way she always does when she's nervous. I might not be good at names, but I'm good at remembering idiosyncrasies. "Alex wants a story on unsolved murders in the county, so I've been doing research on the most interesting ones."

"Why does he want that story?" I ask. "Not enough fresh news to keep him happy?"

"There's never enough fresh news to keep him happy," Gina says, rolling her eyes and shaking her head.

"I take it you're not too fond of your boss?" I ask.

"I'm not going there," Gina says. "I just get frustrated with him and Chris because I think sometimes they forget what it's like to be a reporter. Alex has 15 years worth of contacts. Chris has 25. I have five. Naturally it's going to take me a little longer to get a story than it would take them. I have to do more digging and get people to trust me. I think they forget that people didn't automatically trust them when they started reporting."

"Some people still don't," I say, not being able to pass up an opportunity to slam Alex McIntyre, *The Century's* city editor.

"You think so?" Gina asks.

"I know so," I say, neglecting to mention that the "some people" is me. "Does Alex even know what 'off the record' means?"

"I've asked that question myself," Gina says. "It can be very frustrating when we're talking about a story. I tell him what I know, then say that some of it is off the record and he'll go off on me. It's as if he totally forgot that if one person tells me something, chances are I can get a few more people to tell me as well and someone will go on the record."

"Once upon a time," I say, "I think he knew that. But now that he's got that title after his name he thinks he can bully people into going on the record."

"Exactly. I don't know what makes him think that because he's …"

Gina's ringing cell phone interrupts her. She picks up her purse and starts digging for it, spilling half the contents of her purse - including that notebook - onto the table and the floor. Now she's frustrated because her cell phone connection is bad and half the contents of purse are displayed for the world to see. She tries cramming things back into her purse, while moving around, trying to get better reception. I offer to repack her purse while she goes outside to try to get better reception and finish her call.

I didn't have an ulterior motive for offering. This thought didn't even cross my mind until I touched it. The notebook. I have to look.

Her notes are somewhat cryptic, but I can pick enough out to know that she's digging pretty deep into the Danny Dwyer case, and digging much further than court transcripts and the like.

I get chills down my spine when I see how many times my name is scribbled on just the few pages I've skimmed so far. "Joe Manzarelli?" "Joe M. grand jury testimony" "Joe M. & Kevin Harper" "Joe - how involved?"

Of course there are notes that don't involve me. "Suicide? Why? Who?" "Paramedics" "WV?."

Good questions. The trick will be getting a paramedic, the police or the coroner's office to answer honestly after all these years. And the West Virginia connection? The trail's got to be pretty cold after all this time. I'm fairly certain that after Danny's murder, and the two so-called suicides that came so close after his death, the scumbags from West Virginia that supplied the drugs to this part of the state dropped out of sight.

I need to look more closely at her notebook. I need to know where she's going with this. I slip the notebook into my jacket pocket. I'll take it to my office, make a copy then go to *The Century* parking lot and drop the notebook under her car. She admitted she's scatterbrained. She'll just think she dropped it and didn't notice.

I'm not going to let a reporter from the freakin' *Century* bring me down. Not without a fight. I don't care how pretty her eyes are.

# Chapter Six

I want to spend more time with Gina, but I need to spend as much time with Kathryn as possible, too. Vanessa isn't in her hotel room at all when we call about seven times a night. We leave numerous messages at the desk for her, but she doesn't return them. I'd be concerned had the desk clerk not told me he sees her coming and going all day.

So now Kathryn is a bit depressed. I can't blame her. But I also know I can't leave her with a baby sitter while I go out with Gina. Actually, spending a night at home with Gina and Kathryn might be nice. Maybe with Kathryn around I can forget my obsession with Gina's Danny Dwyer article -- if that's what it is -- and concentrate on getting to know her better.

I decide to make spaghetti for dinner. It's Kathryn's favorite and I've learned you can tell a lot about a woman by how she eats spaghetti. I've actually known women who would go away hungry, leaving an almost full plate of spaghetti, because it's too messy to eat. Seriously. I hope Gina's not one of those.

She's not. I could really fall for a woman who needs three napkins during dinner. But even better than the fact that she likes to eat, and isn't afraid to have sauce on her face, is the fact that she and Kathryn seemed to like each other and have a lot to talk about.

I'm not sure how I feel about both my daughter and the woman I'm interested in being fans of Bon Jovi and the Backstreet Boys, but at least it was a jumping off point for them. I was surprised to learn, through their conversation, that Gina knows quite a bit about swimming and even has a favorite swimmer. Summer Sanders. Seeing as how she's one of Kathryn's favorites as well, even though she was a star before Kathryn was even born, Gina scored major points with my daughter. She scored some points with me as well because now I know that our talk about swimming the other day wasn't contrived. She actually does have an interest in it other than Kathryn.

They're both interested in computers as well. I don't use mine much except for e-mail and to check the latest headlines and weather, but Kathryn would spend hours at the computer if I'd let her. I imagine her mother does let her spend hours at it. A couple weeks ago Kathryn discovered some kind of art program or something called Paint Shop Pro and plays with it quite often. She says that after the Olympics she wants to be a graphic artist and design web pages. Last month she wanted to be a teacher. The month before that, a stock broker. I wouldn't be surprised if tomorrow she decides she wants to be a newspaper reporter.

While Kathryn and Gina play on the computer, I wash dishes and clean up the kitchen and smile. It's been a good night so far. I really like Gina. A lot. It was nice to think about her, talk with her, and get to know her without the Danny Dwyer cloud hanging over my head. Part of it, I'm sure, is the guilt I feel over temporarily confiscating Gina's notebook. I feel so guilty, in fact, that I can't even bring myself to look at the copy I made of it. I wish the Danny Dwyer cloud wasn't there now, but being alone obviously gave me too much time to think. These days, when I'm thinking alone all thoughts seem to turn toward Danny Dwyer.

I decide the best thing to do is join Kathryn and Gina at the computer. I find them playing Pac Man. Kathryn is kicking Gina's butt.

"I'm out of practice," Gina says, after I point out the score.

"Believe it or not, I was good at this in the 80s."

"Weren't we all?" I ask, laughing.

"Everyone I knew was," Gina says.

"You better practice before next time," Kathryn tells Gina.

"It's no fun beating someone this easy."

"Oh really?" Gina says, mussing Kathryn's pixie cut blonde hair. "I just may do that."

"I hate to break this up," I say, "but it's past somebody's bed time."

"Okay Daddy. You sleep well. I'll go to bed when Gina and I are finished playing."

"Kat ...," I say.

"Okay. Okay," she says. "I'm going. I had fun, Gina. I hope you come over again soon."

"I'd like that, Kat," Gina says. "I had fun, too."

Kathryn hugs and kisses me good night then runs off to bed, leaving Gina and me alone in my office. I'm expecting yet another awkward pause, but instead Gina challenges me to a game of Pac Man. I accept, although there's no doubt in my mind I'll be thoroughly embarrassed.

I was in the first game, but I made a miraculous comeback in the second. Gina said Pac Man is kind of like riding a bike. You never forget, it just takes a while to get the hang of it again.

She beat me again in the third game, then quit while she was ahead, rejecting my challenge of a best three out of five match. I turn off the computer and ask if she's tired.

"Is that your way of hinting that you'd like to me leave?" she asks.

"No, not at all," I say. "I just didn't want you to feel as if you had to stay if you'd like to go home."

"I'd rather stay for a while longer if you don't mind," she says. "I've had a really good time and I'm not quite ready for it to end."

"Good," I say. "I'm not ready for it to end yet either."

We decide to watch a video but have a hard time picking out what we'd like to see. I have a hunch it's because she feels the same way about it as I do. It's not so much that we want to watch a movie. It's more like the background noise would be a welcome diversion if our conversation slows down.

"I see there's an Elvis fan in the house," Gina says while looking at my video and DVD collection.

"Is that good or bad?" I ask.

"Very good," she says. "I love Elvis movies."

"Me too," I say, relieved. Believe it or not, an Elvis obsession is a turn-off for some women. I'm glad Gina's not one of them.

"My friends and I used to watch Elvis movies on TV every Sunday," she says.

"Me too," I say. "I remember that Buffalo TV station used to show them at 12:30 every Sunday. After church, my friends and I would watch a movie before we'd go out and play."

"Those were the days, huh?" she says.

"Yeah," I say. "Simple. Elvis and playing with friends. What could be better?"

We decide to watch "Viva Las Vegas!," Gina's favorite, but almost immediately it's clear that we're not actually going to see much of the movie.

Surprisingly enough, we don't need any conversation helpers. We're doing quite well. I do get a little uncomfortable talking about my past because I'm not sure if she's doing research or that she's genuinely interested. I hope I'm making the right move by giving her the benefit of the doubt. I might be dumb when it comes to women, but Vanessa aside, I think I'm a pretty good judge of character and I don't believe Gina is acting.

I believe that so much that I set aside my original plan of shrewdly pumping her for information about her unsolved murders articles. It didn't take me long to realize I really want to get to know her better. The main thing I want to know is why she's unattached. That's baffled me for as long as I've known her. I learn the answer is fairly simple.

Gina had been involved in a couple of serious relationships since college, but her job always seems to interfere in one way or another. The crazy hours, having to jump up and cover a story at a moment's notice, hardly ever being able to make concrete plans all seem to get in the way.

Just like the ringing phone is getting in the way of this conversation. I reluctantly answer it instead of letting the machine pick it up. Habit, I guess.

"What's so important that you have to continually call and leave messages during my vacation?" Vanessa asks.

"Your daughter," I remind her, fuming already. "For some reason, she misses you and, silly me, I thought you might miss her, too."

"Of course I miss her," Vanessa says, not surprisingly slightly slurring her words. "Let me talk to her."

"She's eight years old, Vanessa," I say, disgusted. "It's after 11 p.m. here. She has swim practice in the morning. She's in bed."

"I can never get time zones straight," Vanessa says, laughing. "Let me talk to her anyway. She won't mind."

"No, she probably wouldn't mind," I say. "But I would. Call back tomorrow afternoon and I'll be more than happy to let you talk to her."

"Let me talk to?" Vanessa says. "You'll let me talk to her? I think you're forgetting who has custody of Kathryn."

"I think you're forgetting that since you got custody of her I've spent three times as much time with her as you have, so don't throw that argument at me. Call tomorrow afternoon if you want to talk to her."

I slam the phone down.

"Sorry about that," I say to Gina when I go back to the living room.

"No problem," she says, smiling.

"If you don't mind, I'd like to call it a night. I don't think I'd be very good company right now."

"I understand," she says. "But if you want to talk about it, I'd be more than happy to listen."

"Thanks for the offer, but I don't think talking about it will help."

I walk Gina to her car and open the door for her. When the dome light comes on I notice her notebook on the front passenger seat. I'm glad she found it under her car, where I dropped it after making copies. It makes me feel a little less guilty.

I stand in the driveway watching Gina's car until she turns the corner. I'm still standing in the driveway, wondering what to do next. I need sleep but I'm too worked up to close my eyes. Too many thoughts are racing through my head.

# Chapter Seven

Danny's in the living room, slouched in a chair. His eyes are barely open. He sees me, but I'm not sure if he recognizes me. His clothes look as if he hasn't changed them in days. At least I know he was wearing the same thing two days ago when I saw him last.

His house is filthy and it smells. Beer cans, junk food wrappers and bags, syringes litter the living room. The shades are drawn. The windows are closed. I can almost feel the stale cigarette smoke in the air.

The television is blaring but no one is watching or listening. One of Danny's so-called friends is passed out on the couch; two more are on the floor; another is slumped in a chair. I hear music and voices coming from other rooms in the house. I don't recognize any of them. I don't care who those people are.

I work my way through the maze of trash and stand in front of Danny. He looks up at me and attempts to lift his arm to wave or shake my hand or - I don't know. Something. But his arm drops back down into his lap. He shrugs and closes his eyes. I have to look closely to see that he's actually breathing.

"Danny," I say. "Let's get outta here. Let's go to the lake and just hang out."

"I'm just hangin' here, man," Danny slurs.

"I'm serious," I say. "Let's go someplace. Let's just get outta here."

"Can't man. I'm the host here."

"You need to get out. You at least need some fresh air."

"Don't tell me what I need."

"But you need ….," I start.

"He said don't tell him what he needs," says a woman with sunken in eyes and straggly brown hair. She takes a hit off a joint then passes it to Danny. "He knows what he needs and so do I."

"You're getting me what I really need, aren't you baby?" Danny says to the woman.

"Kevin's getting it ready now," the woman says.

I shake my head.

"You'll be dead by end of the week," I tell Danny as I walk out the door.

I sit bolt upright in bed. I'm in a cold sweat and shaking uncontrollably. That's what the Danny Dwyer nightmare does to me. I find it odd, however, that I always wake up from the nightmare at that point. I never go further. I never go to the point where I see Danny dead in chair with blood dripping from the back of his head.

Maybe I never get to that point in the nightmare because I don't remember exactly how I got to that point in real life, the day it happened. I don't remember much after leaving Danny's house that day. I do remember getting into a fight with someone going into Danny's house as I was leaving. I remember the powerful urge I felt, telling me I needed to get back to Danny's house. I needed to do something. I needed to save him from those people, and himself.

If only - No. I've been saying "if only" for all these years. I can't say it anymore.

I manage to pull myself out of bed. Kathryn won't be up for another two hours and, usually, I'd stay in bed until she wakes me up. But today the last place I want to be is bed. I don't want to risk going back to the nightmare. If this keeps up I may never want to sleep again.

Since the nightmare already ruined my day before it began, I figure looking through the copy I made of Gina's notebook couldn't make matters any worse. When I made the copies, I'd debated making one or two - one for the office and one for home. At first I thought I'd be able to keep this obsession out of the house. But now I'm glad I did make two copies. If the obsession controls my sleep, a few notes around the house won't hurt.

I make a pot of coffee then settle into the reclining chair in my office. I wish I could read Gina's scribbles better. She must have all of this on disk, but the trick will be getting access to it. I suppose I could ask her, but I'm not ready for that yet. First, I need to know how much she knows - or thinks she knows.

She seems to have taken an intense interest in the police chief and coroner. Good place to start. When the official cause of Danny's death was listed as suicide, no one was surprised. I should say no one who relied on rumors, gossip and hearsay was shocked. Suicide was the not-surprising ending to a life that was wasted on drugs. That's how all the "good families" thought.

Danny's father, David Dwyer, seemingly did everything in his power to keep Danny on the straight and narrow path. David Dwyer was the most successful car dealer in the county. He was worth millions. He was respected in the community for all the generous donations he made to civic causes and charities. He was just as generous when it came to his son. He sent Danny off to college in West Virginia, all expenses paid, with a new car and a new credit card. When Danny dropped out after one semester because "it's not my thing, man," his father gave him a job at one of his dealerships and bought him a small, one-story, one-bedroom house.

But it was too late by then. Danny had already fallen in with a dangerous crowd. He dropped all his old friends and started hanging with people who could supply him with drugs. It's possible he was supplying people as well, but not much was ever said about that.

Danny Dwyer's slide, along with his father's heartache and embarrassment, were hot topics around town for quite a while.

That's why no one was surprised that Danny killed himself. Why wouldn't he? What other way out was there for the golden boy turned bad?

But after the initial ruling of suicide, David Dwyer was furious. He called *The Century* and demanded they do a follow-up story on how a gunshot wound to the back of the head could be ruled suicide.

After one story, which included statements from the police chief and coroner simply saying the case was closed, *The Century* dropped the story. Bill Valentine said essentially the same thing. If the police call it a suicide and there's no one to charge with the crime, his office doesn't have anything to do with it. All the paramedics on the scene would say was "no comment."

But David Dwyer didn't give up that easily.

He wrote to his Congressman, Senator, state representatives, all his justice system contacts, anyone he could think of. For 18 months he was relentless. In the meantime, the police chief resigned for "personal reasons" and the coroner left town to take another job.

The new police chief reopened the case almost immediately, ruled Danny's death a homicide and started the investigation. Although a grand jury was convened, there weren't any indictments.

As far as I know, the case is still open but I doubt the investigation is active. Why would it be? Danny's parents died several years ago in a car accident. He didn't have any other close relatives and he died pretty much friendless so there isn't anyone to put pressure on the police to continue the investigation. The few friends Danny did have left, myself included, simply want to put that chapter of our lives behind us.

I wish *The Century* would let it be as well. They didn't want the story then. What's the point of bringing it up now?

# Chapter Eight

Kathryn talked me into asking Gina out to dinner and a movie. After the call from her mother, she decided she wanted to spend the night at a friend's house and she didn't want me home alone. Good idea. Alone time equals thinking time.

I'm a bit nervous when I call Gina to ask her out on such short notice. But I'm thrilled when she accepts.

We decide to go to Gilbert's, a quiet Italian place in Warren, 45 minutes outside of town. Neither of us wants the Brafferd rumor mill turning just yet. After a couple hours I realize I can't tease Gina anymore about losing track of time. It's so easy losing track of time when I'm with her. Even if we left for the theater right now we'd miss the start of the movie. We decide the later show would be fine, but we miss that as well.

And we haven't even started talking about Danny Dwyer yet.

Before I left my house to pick Gina up I decided the best thing to do for my peace of mind is ask her what exactly she's doing with the article.

I'm happy to learn that she doesn't want anything to do with the story, but she doesn't have a choice. She does admit that she's drawing out the research part longer than she would for any other story because she's hoping something big will turn up and she'll be assigned to that story instead.

She also admits that she's been warned to be very careful.

"My Mom's Uncle George was sheriff at the time," Gina says. "He told me I don't want any part of this. When I told him I didn't have a choice, he told me to be very careful and to be very careful about what I write."

"Nothing more specific than that?" I ask.

"No. I'm surprised I got that much out of him. As soon as I said the name Danny Dwyer his eyes bugged open and he started his warnings."

"Interesting," I say.

"Uh huh. Any theories?"

"Nope. You?"

"No."

"So, where do you go from here?" I ask.

"No clue. Well, I know where I want to go, but I'm afraid."

"Where? Why?"

"Well, I want to ask you why you were called to testify before the grand jury."

"Why were you afraid?" I ask, still trying to decide if I'll answer her question and, if I won't, how to tactfully get out of it.

"Well, I sense that you're really uncomfortable talking about this and I didn't want to make you uncomfortable. I'm having a great time with you ... not just today, but for the past few weeks ... and I don't want to do anything to change that."

"I've been having a great time, too. And I'm really glad you are."

"But are you going to answer my question?" she asks, flashing that addictive smile.

"I am uncomfortable," I say, "but can talk about it. What do you want to know?"

"What did you tell the grand jury?"

"Not much really," I say. "They asked me a lot about why Danny and I grew apart. I told it was because he was into drugs. I wasn't."

"That's it?"

"They asked me where I was the day Danny died."

"And?"

"I don't remember much about that day. What I do remember is a blur. I saw Danny late that morning. I saw him very late that night after the police were already at his house. I can't remember what happened during the hours in between."

"You don't remember anything? No one remembers seeing you?" Gina asks.

No. And no."

"Have you thought about some kind of therapy or hypnosis or something to help you remember?"

"What if I don't want to remember?"

"Do you?"

"Sometimes. Sometimes I just want to forget the whole mess ever happened. Sometimes," I say, looking off into the distance, "I want to forget I ever knew Danny Dwyer."

"That's got to make you sad."

"It does I suppose. But no sadder than the fact my best friend died a drug-related death."

"That's why you don't represent drug offenders, isn't it?" Gina asks.

"Yep. I didn't always operate that way though. I thought if I could get them early, like on their first offense, I could give them free counseling as well as legal representation. I was naïve enough to think they could and would learn from my experience. But it didn't work out that way. I kept seeing most of these people over and over. It wore me out and broke me down. So rather than pick and choose and only represent the people I thought I could change, I chose to not represent any drug offenders at all."

"Have you ever thought about giving lectures at schools or working with the police's D.A.R.E. program?" Gina asks.

"For a brief moment," I say. "But then I decided I wanted to put the whole thing behind me. While there's still a cloud over Danny's death I want to distance myself as much as possible. You know as well as I do that in this county if there's even a perception of impropriety, no one takes you seriously. Most people around here have forgotten about Danny Dwyer. Or they don't care. I don't want to jog anyone's memory."

"I guess I can understand that," Gina says, reaching across the table and touching my hand.

I smile. Her touch feels good. Comforting. Safe.

We decide to call it a night. It's amazing how much a heavy conversation can take out of you. As we're leaving the restaurant, one of the elderly ladies who had been sitting at a table near us stops us.

"I heard you talking about David Dwyer and his son," the woman says.

I don't say anything. I mean, what should I say?

"Is there anything new about the death of his poor son?" the woman asks.

"No, not really," I say.

"That's too bad," the woman says. "Poor, poor man. He and my dear late husband spent many a night talking about his troubles. First there's the trouble with his business, then that terrible mess with his son. It's almost a blessing that he and his dear wife died in that car accident."

"Trouble with his business?" I ask, totally unaware that David Dwyer had any problems with the car dealership.

"Oh yes," the woman says. "It was quite a struggle. I don't know any of the details. All I know is that he kept saying to my husband 'the bastard is going to ruin me.' I don't know who he meant and I figured if my husband wanted me to know he would have told me."

"Very interesting," I say.

"Just the ramblings of an old woman," the woman says, smiling. "You kids go and have a good night."

"We will," I say, watching her walk away. Then I just say "Hmmmm?"

"Hmmmm what?" Gina asks.

"It's just interesting," I say. "That's all."

# Chapter Nine

Chinese food usually makes me feel better. It sort of heals all my wounds. That's why I thought lunch at The Rice Bowl was just what I needed. But there's nothing like Alex McIntyre and Chris Palmer, two of The Century's editors, to ruin a good plan.

They're sitting at the booth next to mine at the restaurant. You'd think the partial wall between the booths would shield me from their loud, annoying voices, but my luck hasn't been going that way lately.

Of course I can't help but eavesdrop. At first their conversation is boring, not even worth listening in on. But then they start talking about Gina and my ears perk up again.

"Is she really doing that much research," Chris asks, "or is she dragging her feet because she doesn't want to do the story?"

"From what I've seen, she doing that much research," Alex says.

"What has she found out so far?" Chris asks.

"I'm not sure. We haven't talked about it that much," Alex says. "This was more of an assignment from you, not me."

"Are you telling me I should be the one jumping on her ass to get it done?"

"Not exactly," Alex says. "I know that's my job. But you're more into it than I am. You also know more of the history than I do. You covered the original story, after all. I was in high school 300 miles away when Dwyer was killed."

"You're right, I do know more of the history and I don't think it should be taking her this long to do research. Do you think it has anything to do with Manzarelli?"

"Why would you ask that?"

"She's obviously got a thing for him," Chris says. "Do you think that would have anything to do with her procrastination?"

"You mean do I think she's drawing it out so she can spend more time with him?" Alex asks.

"No. I mean do you think she's dragging this out, hoping we'll forget about the story so she won't have to drag Manzarelli's name through the mud?"

"Why would that happen?" Alex asks.

"You really don't know anything about this case, do you?" Chris asks. "Manzarelli was at the murder scene with blood on his hands and clothes."

"No way!" Alex says.

Oh shit, I think as I start paying even closer attention to the their conversation. My "I don't remember" defense isn't going to hold much longer if this gets out. Until now, I'd totally forgotten that Chris got her hands on that piece of information.

"Why didn't I know that before?" Alex asks. "It was never in the paper was it? Tell me more. Tell me more."

"No, it was never in the paper," Chris says. "I was dating a cop at the time and one night we were talking about the murder and he happened to blurt out that Manzarelli was a suspect. I couldn't get anyone to confirm so I couldn't print it."

"Holy shit," Alex says. "I had no idea. Does Gina know?"

"I don't know. It's always been the newspaper's policy not to keep notes after a story's been printed, so there's nothing in the files about it. But if I found out, and if other people know about it, there's a possibility Gina knows, too."

"I can't believe she would have found that information and not mentioned anything about it to me," Alex says.

I can't either, I think. Now I can't help but wonder if she's using me to get a story.

"That's why I'm concerned about her little crush on Manzarelli," Chris says. "This could be a good story. I don't want her blowing it or sugar coating it because of her feelings for him. Imagine how good this story will be if she can get someone to confirm Manzarelli's involvement."

"That would be a great story," Alex says. "A lawyer who won't defend drug users involved in a drug-related murder. Doesn't get much better than that."

"Exactly," Chris says. "Now let's make sure she doesn't blow it."

This is much worse than I thought, I think as Chris and Alex's conversation changes gears. I'd always had a feeling Chris and Alex didn't like me, but I didn't think they'd try to hang me out to dry - and use Gina to do it.

At least from the sound of things Gina isn't in on it. But I still have to wonder how much she knows. If she knows about the blood on my hands and clothes, why hasn't she asked me yet? If she doesn't know, what will she think and how will she treat me when and if she does find out?

If? From what I just heard, there's no "if" about it. Alex and Chris will make sure she knows. I'll just have to find a way to make sure I tell her first and hope that makes a difference.

# Chapter Ten

I didn't expect to see Gina at the courthouse today and, to be honest, I really don't want to talk to her. I'm still a little shaken up by the Alex and Chris conversation and I'm sure Gina would notice something's wrong. I'm not ready to talk to her about that yet.

I hope she doesn't see me. I just need to get to the law library, look something up and get out of here. I don't need to talk to anyone, least of all Gina.

Good. Bill Valentine has her cornered. She could be there for hours. I hear her telling him she's at the courthouse because she has an interview with Judge Vaughn in half an hour concerning the upcoming election.

I was wrong about Valentine keeping Gina cornered for hours. I wasn't in the law library for ten minutes before he walked in.

"Mr. Manzarelli," he says. "I just had a chat with your girlfriend."

"I don't have a girlfriend," I say, partially because I'm not sure if Gina could be classified as my girlfriend; partially just to be argumentative.

"Well then, I had a chat with Gina Hamilton. Very interesting chat I might add."

"I'm sure it was," I say, hoping that if I act as if I'm not interested he'll go away.

"Seems she has an interest in the murder," Valentine says.

"The murder?" I say, pretending I don't know what he's talking about.

"Dwyer."

"Oh, I see."

"Yes. Very interesting chat. Very interesting chat indeed," Valentine says as he walks out of the room.

"Asshole," I whisper after he's gone.

The last thing I need right now is Bill Valentine on my ass even more than he has been since the day I started practicing law in Brafferd County.

\*\*\*\*\*\*\*\*\*\*

So much for not wanting to run into Gina today. Although we left the courthouse through different doors, we ended up in the parking lot at the same time. I pretend I don't see her, but it doesn't work.

"Fancy meeting you here," she says, as we unlock our car doors.

"Hi there," I say. "What brings you to the courthouse today?"

"I was supposed to have an interview with Judge Vaughn, but he postponed at the last minute."

"That sucks - making the drive all the way over here for nothing."

"Yeah," she says. "It was kind of strange, too. Judge Vaughn was walking into his outer office at the same time I got there. We chatted for a few minutes, he told me he was looking forward to the interview, his secretary told him Bill Valentine needed to speak with him immediately, then he went into his office. Not more than a minute later, he came back out, told me he had to postpone the interview and left."

"That is strange," I say.

"I guess I'll have to keep my eyes open for a new story," she says. "Ya never know."

"That's right," I say. "Ya never know."

"Are you okay?" she asks. "You're acting as if something's bothering you."

"I'm fine," I lie. "Don't worry about me, okay?"

"Okay."

"See ya soon," I say, getting into my car. I can't even look back at her in my rearview mirror because I know I hurt her feelings and I don't want to see the look on her face.

I promise myself I'll make it up to her soon, but not tonight. I have, of all things, a PTA meeting to attend. One of us has to do it and PTA doesn't quite fit into Vanessa's schedule.

I have to stop thinking about Vanessa. I'm in a bad enough mood without adding her to the mix.

Since I'm already in a bad mood, I decide I might as well spend the couple of hours before the PTA meeting looking through the copy of Gina's notebook.

I can't concentrate on anything she's written. It's mostly just names anyway. Paramedics. Police officers. Neighbors. I don't know how she's going to get any information out of any of those people. If investigations couldn't do it, and if nothing came out during grand jury testimony, what makes her think anyone's going to tell her anything?

The more I look at the copy of the notebook, the guiltier I feel, not just for temporarily confiscating the notebook, but for the way I treated Gina this afternoon.

I'm also afraid of what her reaction will be when and if Alex and Chris tell her what they talked about concerning my involvement in the murder. "My involvement in the murder." That even sounds bad. How bad will it sound when Alex and Chris tell her about the blood on my clothes and hands? I think it would be best for everyone if she heard that from me.

I think the only way I'm going to rid myself of this guilt and burden is to call her right now.

Figures. Answering machine. I'm prepared - well, semi-prepared - to talk to her, not her machine, so I hang up. I could call her cell phone. No. I guess I'm not as prepared as I thought I was. I compose myself, then press in her number again. I don't know why I'm shaking as I listen to her message on the machine. I recompose myself enough to leave a message at the beep.

"There's something I need to tell you about the Danny Dwyer case," I say into the phone. "You might have heard about this already. If you have I'd like to try to explain. If you haven't, I'd like you to hear it from me. I also wanted to apologize for my behavior this afternoon. I'm going out now, but I'll be home around 9 if you'd like to call or come over."

I hang up and sigh. I don't know how I'm going to explain the blood. I don't know how it got there.

# Chapter Eleven

Gina didn't seem upset at all about the way I treated her this afternoon. Instead, she seemed concerned that something was weighing heavily on my mind. She seemed sincere in her offer to help, so I'll do my best to try and let her help.

I tell her in great deal about the last time I saw Danny alive, and apologize to her for not telling her all of this the night we went to dinner and talked about my grand jury testimony. I explain why it's easier to say "I don't remember," than to have all those memories come flooding back.

I tell her about honestly not being able to remember anything between the time I left Danny's house and returned to find him dead. I tell her about the looks on the faces of the police officers when they saw the blood on my hands and clothes, and how scared I was.

"Didn't you say you got into a fight with someone outside of Danny's house?" Gina asks.

I nod.

"Well, couldn't the blood have come from that?"

"That's what I like to think. I guess that's what a lot of people thought. I was dangerously close to being indicted but, because of the fight, there was that little bit of doubt. You have to remember this was way before DNA testing, so the police didn't have that option."

"You were close to being indicted?" she asks incredulously.

"That's what Bill Valentine tells me ... over and over and over."

"Still? After all these years?"

"Not as much as he used to," I say, "but he still brings it up every now and then."

"Why would he do that?"

"I don't know," I say. "Maybe he still believes I'm guilty. Maybe he doesn't like me. Maybe he's just an asshole. I really don't know."

"Ya know, Chris doesn't like him all that much either," Gina says.

"Really? I didn't know that."

"Yeah. She never says why she doesn't like him, just that she doesn't."

"Well, she doesn't like me either, and I have no idea if it's because of Danny."

"The best way to put this whole thing to rest," she says, "is to find out who really killed Danny Dwyer."

"Simple as that, huh?" I ask, amazed at how easy she makes it sound.

"We can do it."

"We?"

"Sure. I think we'd make a pretty good team, don't you?"

I swear she's blushing and probably for the same reason I am. Despite the serious nature of our conversation, there's a definite undertone. I wouldn't go as far as to say it's sexual, but it's something.

"Yes, I think we would make a good team," I say. "What do you have in mind?"

She's blushing again, but manages to stick to the subject at hand.

"First of all," she says, "I think we should try to contact everyone you saw at Danny's house that day."

"I only knew one person," I say. "I have no clue how to get in touch with any of those people."

"You know one person," she says. "That's a start."

# Chapter Twelve

I don't know where to start the search for Kevin Harper, but I know it has to be done. I ask my secretary Barbara to help me. There are a lot of paths to follow and I'm sure we'll come across a lot of dead ends. It'll be much easier having two people on the trail.

Besides, I still have clients to contend with and a daughter to worry about.

Now that Vanessa's back in town, Kathryn is living with her again. Poor Kat. She calls me and e-mails me every evening telling me how lonely she is. Apparently there's been an endless stream of baby-sitters for Kat as Vanessa paints the town with an endless stream of men.

Clearly, Vanessa's choice of baby-sitters hasn't been so hot either. From what Kathryn tells me, in not so many words, they're simply younger versions of Vanessa. They're more interested in their boyfriends than they are about spending time with Kat. My daughter's after school life since Vanessa returned from Cancun has pretty much consisted of dinner delivered from Pizza Hut, playing on the computer and watching television. On nights that Vanessa or a baby-sitter has time for her, Kathryn gets treated to Taco Bell or Subway.

I'm amazed that Vanessa finds time to get Kathryn to swim practice. I'm sure that has more to do with Kathryn's persistence than any kind of maternal instinct Vanessa has hidden away somewhere.

I promise myself that as soon as I find and talk to Kevin Harper, I'll plan something special with Kathryn. I would drop everything and do it now, but I'm so preoccupied that I know she'd be disappointed that my mind was someplace else. She's much too perceptive for me to even attempt hiding my preoccupation from her.

But finally, some good luck headed my way.

Much to my surprise, finding Kevin Harper wasn't has hard as I thought it would be and only took a few hours. I knew he was a registered student at the local university at the time of Danny's death, so Barbara started searching there. Amazingly enough, instead of simply dropping out of college, Kevin transferred and the local university had a record of the transfer.

I'm not surprised to learn he moved back home to Elkins, West Virginia, and enrolled at Elkins and Davis College. I am amazed to learn, however, that he graduated with a degree in business. The college's current alumni directory doesn't have a job listing for him, but it does have a home address and phone number.

I decide a personal visit would be much more productive than a phone call. If I called and he didn't want to talk he could hang up on me, not answer his phone again and get an unlisted number so I'd never bother him again. If I just show up, he won't be able to get away.

One of the things Kathryn did teach me how to do on the computer is find maps. I look for Elkins and discover it's just straight down Route 219 so getting there shouldn't be a problem at all. The Mapquest directions would probably get me there faster, but my brain is so full that a simple "follow 219" is about all I can handle right now. At any rate, I can probably drive down and back in one day if I leave early enough in the morning.

I debate on whether to tell Gina I'm going to West Virginia. I guess I should let her know so she won't worry about me. I don't think I'm overestimating her feelings for me by thinking she'd worry. I truly believe she would. I know I'd worry about her if she disappeared without a trace for a day or two.

I explain to her how I found Kevin and my rationale for driving to West Virginia instead of simply calling him. She congratulates me and agrees that it's better to confront him in person.

She says she'd offer to go with me, but there's no way she could get off work on such short notice. I tell her I understand, but I don't tell her it's probably for the best. I'd rather do this alone anyway. I think the drive time will do me a lot of good, give me some time to get my thoughts together. I have no idea what I'm going to say when I confront Kevin Harper.

I'm a different person than I was then. I assume he is as well. We never did like each other, so any kind of meeting with him would be unpleasant. A meeting to talk about Danny's death could be downright wretched.

After talking with Gina on the phone, I drive over to Vanessa's house to see Kathryn. Not surprisingly, Vanessa's not home. Good. I didn't want to see her anyway.

The baby-sitter doesn't even acknowledge my presence. She's involved in a very animated telephone conversation while watching a rerun of "Friends" on television. Just as well. I didn't want to talk to her either.

Kathryn and I go to her bedroom, where she has me read the composition she just finished for English. We play a couple of games of Pac Man. She shows me her new swimsuit. All in all, it was a nice visit.

I tell Kathryn I have to go out of town for a couple of days, make sure she has my cell phone number, then give her a tight hug before leaving.

Back at my house, I take a shower, pack a few things in an overnight bag then plop down onto the bed. I try closing my eyes but it doesn't work. I can't stop staring at the ceiling while thoughts of Danny, Kevin and a million other things race through my head.

After about an hour of tossing, turning and checking the clock, I decide I might as well start the trip to West Virginia now. Maybe driving at night will make me tired enough to sleep and I can stop at a motel along the way.

\*\*\*\*\*\*\*\*\*\*

I get to Elkins at just after 7 a.m. I decide it's too early to go to Kevin's house, so I look for someplace to have coffee - someplace other than a convenience store and in something other than a

Styrofoam cup.

I find a diner on a corner and decide it looks pleasant enough. I sit at the counter and order a cup of coffee. At first I hadn't thought about food, but when the waitress brings biscuits and gravy to the man sitting next to me, it smells so good I can't resist.

Eating was a good idea. After the biscuits, gravy and scrambled eggs I feel much more human. It also killed some time. Eight o'clock is a far more acceptable time for an unexpected visit than seven.

I ask the waitress for directions to Jackson Avenue, where Kevin lives. I'm surprised to learn that it's less than three blocks from the diner. I'm a little nervous, too, because I'm not quite ready to confront Kevin. I was hoping to have a little more driving and thinking time.

I drive slowly down Jackson Avenue, looking closely at the numbers on the houses. My heart skips a beat when I see Kevin's house. I park across the street and just stare. After two minutes, which seemed more like two hours, I muster up enough nerve to walk up to the house and knock on the door.

It wasn't as hard as I thought it would be. A woman I assume is his wife told me Kevin is at work and gives me directions without even asking who I am or what I want. All for the best.

Here we go again.

# Chapter Thirteen

I pull into the lot of WV Quality Cars, the car dealership where Kevin's wife told me he works. Immediately, a salesman asks if I need help. He looks disappointed when I tell him I'm looking for Kevin, but points me in the direction of the office.

Before anyone asks me, or before I need to ask, I see a nameplate on one of the doors in the office/showroom. It reads "Kevin Harper Business Manager." Now that is a surprise. Although I know he has a degree in business from Elkins and Davis, I assumed he was a mechanic or possibly a salesman. My heart is pounding as I knock on the door. A man's voice inside tells me to come in.

He's barely changed a bit. He's filled out a little, not nearly as sickeningly thin. His eyes aren't bloodshot. He's clean and his hair is combed. But it's Kevin Harper, without a doubt.

I can tell by the shocked look on his face that he recognizes me, too.

Now what? I didn't have to wait long for the answer.

"Joe Manzarelli," Kevin says, standing up from behind his desk. "If you aren't a blast from the past."

"Kevin," I say, extending my hand. "How are ya?"

"Fine," he says, briefly shaking my hand. "How did you find me here ... and a better question is why?"

"How isn't important," I say. "Why is that I need some answers about Danny."

"That book's been closed for a long time," Kevin says. "I'd rather not reopen it."

"I would have rather not reopened it either," I say, "but it's being reopened anyway. I need some answers before it can be closed once and for all. Don't you want to know who killed Danny?"

"I'd rather leave it alone."

"Please Kevin," I say, one step from begging, which I refuse to do no matter how difficult this becomes. "I just need to ask you a few questions."

"What kind of questions?"

"About the day Danny died."

"You ask. I'll answer what I can, but I don't remember much."

Sounds familiar, I think to myself.

"I don't even know where to start," I say. "I guess I need to know if you remember anything at all unusual, seeing anyone out of the ordinary, right before Danny died."

"Nope," Kevin says, not looking me in the eye for the first time since I stepped into his office.

"Nothing? Nothing at all?"

"No," he says, looking out the window. "Danny was a little more out of it than usual, but I heard from someone that he had a run-in with his father earlier in the day so I thought it had something to do with that."

"Any idea what the run-in was about?" I ask.

"The usual," Kevin says. "Danny was an embarrassment to his father and he was killing the old man's business."

"How could Danny be killing the business?" I ask.

"I guess people didn't want to do business with someone whose son is a drug addict," Kevin says, shrugging. "I really didn't get into Danny's personal life. It was all business with us. As long as he kept my customer base stable, I didn't much care about anything else. Sounds cold and heartless now, but I was a different person then."

"Danny kept your customer base stable?" I ask.

"He was my best salesman up in your neck of the woods," Kevin says.

"I didn't know that," I say. "I thought he was just using. I didn't know he was selling."

"How do you think he got the money to buy?" Kevin asks, looking at me again. "He wasn't running the show though."

"Who was?"

"Don't know."

"I think you do," I say, judging by the look on Kevin's face.

"I think I've answered all the questions I'm going to answer."

"Okay. Okay," I say. "I won't ask about that anymore. But I do have a couple more ..."

"I said no more."

"I just need to know if you were there when Danny died."

"Like I said," he says, looking out the window again. "No more questions."

"You were there, weren't you?"

He keeps staring out the window but doesn't answer.

"This is going to sound crazy," I say, "but ... It wasn't me was it?"

"You don't know?" Kevin says, looking at me again and starting to laugh. "You don't remember if you killed your best friend?"

"No. I don't. I remember leaving the house and I remember seeing Danny dead after the police got there. I don't remember anything in between."

Kevin shakes his head.

"No man," Kevin says. "You didn't kill Danny."

"That means you know who did."

"Enough questions. I think you should leave."

Seeing as I'm probably not going to get any further with him, I decide he's probably right. I thank him for his time and leave. Neither of us offered our hands to shake.

If I can believe him, at least now I know for sure that I didn't kill Danny.

\*\*\*\*\*\*\*\*\*\*

I drive down to that diner to pick up a cup of coffee for the road, but before I go in I call Gina and tell her what I learned.

"Thank God," she says after I tell her Kevin says I didn't kill Danny. "That's got to be a huge load off your mind."

"You can't imagine," I say. "But I wish I could have gotten him to tell me who did. I think he knows. No. I know he knows."

"Well," she says. "Look at it this way. He wouldn't be covering it up if the persons wasn't still alive and … "

"And if he wasn't afraid this person would find out he talked," I finish.

"Exactly."

"I guess that's something to go on," I say.

"It's better than nothing."

"I guess you're right," I say. "So, how's it going on your end?"

"Believe it or not, it's pretty close to how it's going on your end. I talked to the former police chief. Well, let's say I had a meeting with the former police chief. He's scared to death of talking about this. He's covering something up but I can't get a handle on what it is."

"Tell ya what," I say. "I'll be home in less than eight hours if everything goes as planned. When I get back we can put our heads together and figure out where to go from here."

\*\*\*\*\*\*\*\*\*\*\*

I run through my conversation with Kevin over and over and over. There's got to be some kind of clue in there to point me in the right direction. If only I could put my finger on it.

So much for everything going as planned. I just came across an accident and traffic is stopped while it gets cleaned up. I stare out the window at another WV Quality Cars dealership and think it's ironic that Kevin now works at a car dealership, the same line of work as Danny's father.

After about 45 minutes waiting for the police to let us go, I'm on my way home again. Before I cross the state line between West Virginia and Pennsylvania, I drive past two more WV Quality Cars lots. I can't figure out why that strikes me as odd.

# Chapter Fourteen

"He was scared, I'm tellin' ya," Gina says, as we sit in my living room eating Pringles and sipping red wine. "It wasn't so much that he didn't want to tell me as he was afraid to tell me."

"You're sure?" I ask.

"I could see it in his eyes," she says. "It's almost like if I guessed things, he would have been thrilled to tell me I was right. But I couldn't get enough from him to even guess."

"Did you get to talk about his grand jury testimony at all?" I ask.

"Oh man, you're not gonna believe this," she says. "They hardly asked him anything! They asked what time he got there, what he saw and what time he called the coroner. They asked why he didn't call for an investigation. He told them he didn't think it was necessary. That was it. Can you believe that?"

"He says a gunshot to the back of the head is suicide, and no one can think to ask him why?"

"Unbelievable, huh?"

"It's unreal," I say. "I wonder who he's afraid of. I wonder if he's afraid of the same person Kevin Harper is afraid of."

"Person or people," Gina says. "Let's not count out the possibility that more than one person is involved in this cover-up."

"It probably makes more sense that there's more than one person involved," I say. "We don't even know what we're dealing with yet and it seems fairly complicated."

"Did you ever see 'All the President's Men?'" Gina asks.

"Yeah. Why?"

"Remember when Deep Throat tells Bob Woodward to follow the money?"

"Woodward was Robert Redford, right?"

"Yes, but that's beside the point. Remember that?"

"No, but tell me what you're getting at."

"Kevin mentioned something about Danny killing his father's business, right?"

"Right."

"And that woman at the restaurant mentioned something about David Dwyer's business failing, right?"

"Right."

"There's a lot of money in drug dealing, right?"

"Right."

"Those two things seem unconnected right now, but if we find a connection I bet we'll be closer to finding out who killed Danny and why. I think our best bet to find that connection would be to follow the money."

"That sounds easy enough," I say, "but the money trail's got to be ice cold by now."

"You thought that about Kevin Harper and you found him, didn't you?"

I smile. "You believe anything's possible if you try hard enough, don't you?"

"Sure," Gina says. "Don't you?"

"No," I say, laughing. "Not at all."

"That's sad."

"I prefer to think of it as realistic."

"But if you don't believe anything's possible, how can you have dreams?"

"Who says I have dreams?"

"You don't have dreams? How can you live without having dreams?"

"I dream about Kathryn's life. I dream good things for her. I dream that she'll get everything she hopes for. But as for me, I stopped dreaming a long time ago."

"I don't believe you," she says.

"Well, every now and then I might let a daydream slip in, but I try not to concentrate on it. I've had too many disappointments in my life to think any of them will ever come true now."

"That's a very sad and depressing way to lead your life, Mr. Manzarelli."

"You get used to it," I say. "So, Gina of *The Century*, how did we get onto this topic anyway?"

"I don't remember," she says, shrugging and laughing, "but I assume you'd like to change topics?"

"I'd like that very much. I think we need a more specific game plan than 'follow the money.'"

"Do you have anything in mind?"

"I think I should concentrate on finding out all I can about David Dwyer's business. You should keep doing what you're doing, talking to police, paramedics, whoever you can get to talk. Someone's bound to slip up and say something eventually."

"Sounds like a good plan to me."

"Glad you like it," I say. "So, are you tired? I'm beat."

"In other words, 'Hit the road Gina,'" she says, laughing again.

I can't get over how much I love her laugh.

"You can stay if you like," I say. "You must be pretty tired, too, and Kathryn's room is free."

"Are you sure it wouldn't be inconvenient?"

"Not inconvenient at all," I say. "And having someone to talk to in the morning would be nice."

"Hmmm?" she says. "Thinking about something in the future that would be nice. Sounds like a daydream to me, counselor."

I pick up a throw pillow from the couch and toss it at her.

"I thought we dropped that subject," I say.

"Okay. I'll stop," she says, winking.

"Good," I say. "So, are you going to stay?"

"If you're sure you don't mind, I think I will. I just thought about driving home, and it wasn't pretty. I think I'm a little more tired than I thought I was."

"I'm absolutely positive I don't mind," I say. "So, are you ready to call it a night?"

She nods, I show her the way to Kathryn's bedroom and bathroom and tell her to make herself at home.

"I don't have an extra toothbrush," I say, "but feel free to use anything else in Kathryn's bathroom or mine that you need."

"Thank you, I will. And don't worry about the toothbrush. I always carry one with me."

"You always carry a toothbrush?"

"On some days I'm away from home all day," she says. "I don't want my mouth and teeth feeling and looking all gross. I wouldn't want to be interviewing someone like, say, the governor after working for six or seven hours and have his first impression of me be bad breath or a piece of spinach stuck to my tooth."

"Good point," I say. "I'm surprised you don't carry deodorant, too."

"I do," she says. "Can't have the governor thinking I stink."

God, she's cute, I think to myself.

"Okay Gina of *The Century*," I say, standing in the door of Kathryn's bedroom. "I'll see you in the morning."

"Night Joe," she says. "And thank you for offering to let me stay here tonight."

"No problem," I say, as I walk down the hall to my bedroom.

I knew I was tired, but I didn't realize I was this tired until I sat on my bed. I feel as if I could sleep for a week. I'm surprised I have enough energy to pull my socks off. I'm pretty sure I don't have enough energy left to do much more than that. I slip myself under the sheets, still with my jeans and polo shirt on, then pull the sheets and comforter over me.

I can't believe I have a beautiful, intelligent woman who obviously likes me right down the hall and I can't even keep my eyes open.

# Chapter Fifteen

"I hope you don't mind that I snooped around and helped myself to the coffee," Gina says, standing in my kitchen in her bare feet wearing jeans and a white T-shirt. "I made enough for both of us."

"No, not at all," I say, still trying to wake up. I'm not used to having someone have coffee ready for me in the morning. Not even Vanessa did that.

She pours some coffee into my "World's Best Dad" cup and hands it to me.

"Thanks," I say, taking the cup squinting while I look at her.

"That's not what you were wearing last night."

"Toothpaste, deodorant and a change of clothes," she says.

"You're scaring me, Gina," I say, attempting a smile. "You carry a change of clothes with you, too?"

"Yes. What if I'm all dressed up for court or an important meeting, then I have to change gears and go cover an accident in the forest or someplace dirty and hard to get to? I can't be trudging through the woods in high heels and a skirt, can I?"

"I guess not," I say.

"Boy Scouts aren't the only ones who are always prepared," she says. "I may be scatterbrained, but I'm usually ready for anything."

"Are you always this talkative and cheerful in the morning?" I ask, sitting at the kitchen table.

"Not always," she says, "but usually."

"And that's your first cup of coffee?"

"Yes."

"Now you're really scaring me." I wink at her, then take a sip of coffee.

She sits across from me at the table.

"What do you have planned for the day?" she asks. "Are you going to be able to concentrate on David Dwyer's business, or do you have something else?"

"I should tie up some loose ends with a few clients before I start on the Dwyer thing," I say, "but I'm not sure if I'll be able to concentrate on anything else. I want to get this over with once and for all. Maybe I'll dedicate the morning to my clients then start on Dwyer after lunch."

"Sounds good," she says.

"How 'bout you?" I ask. "What do you have planned?"

"I have a meeting today," she says. "It's at two this afternoon, so it totally screws up my day. I can't get very involved in anything because I'll have to stop for the meeting. By the time the meeting's over, it'll be getting close to evening when it's harder to get a hold of people I need to talk to. ... But you don't want to hear me whine. You want to hear what I have planned."

"Number one," I say, "I don't think you were whining. Number two, I never mind listening to you talk about anything. Number three, yes, I'd like to hear what you have planned."

"Thanks," she says, a slight blush in her cheeks. "My plan for the day is to try and talk to some police officers and paramedics. I hope I can get at least one person to tell me something. There's got to be someone out there who's not afraid to talk."

"You would think so, wouldn't you? I guess we'll find out."

"I hope so," she says. "But I'm not going to find out anything if I don't get moving. I should really get home, shower and put on some clean clothes."

"Good start," I say.

Gina smiles, then leaves the kitchen. I follow her to Kathryn's bedroom, where she's stuffing a few of her personal items back into her purse and backpack, which I assume she keeps in her car. I didn't hear her go out to get it last night but, then again, I didn't hear anything after my head hit the pillow.

"Thanks for letting me spend the night," she says, as she starts walking toward the front door of the house.

"No," I say. "Thank you for staying. It was nice to have someone to share my morning coffee with."

"That was nice," she says, her hand on the doorknob. I don't want her to go. I want to kiss her, then spend the rest of the day kissing her and talking and kissing her some more. "Maybe we can do that again sometime … have coffee together, I mean."

"I'd like that very much."

"I guess I should go," she says.

"I guess," I say, but wanting nothing more than for her to stay. "Lunch. … Do you have any plans for lunch?"

"Not yet."

"Good. Want to get together?"

"That would be great," she says, smiling.

"Meet me in front of *The Century* building at noon?"

"Sounds great to me," she says. "See ya at noon."

I smile as I watch her walk to her car, toss her purse and backpack inside then drive away. Now that I know she's not out to get me, it's much easier to admit to myself that I'm really falling for her.

\*\*\*\*\*\*\*\*\*\*

It's only a few blocks from my office to Gina's and, since it's a nice day, I decide to walk. I didn't accomplish anything on the Dwyer front this morning because my clients needed more attention than I'd anticipated. But I can tell from a few hundred feet away that Gina must have some new information.

Her eyes are sparkling, she's smiling and she's practically bouncing as she paces in front of the building.

"Let me guess," I say, as I get closer to her. "You're in a good mood."

"I have some pretty interesting stuff to tell you," she says in an almost singsong tone. "This is good."

"I can hardly wait," I say. "Is The Corner okay for lunch?"

"Sounds good to me," she says.

She tells me she'd rather not tell me what she found out until we

67

get to the restaurant so, instead, I tell her about my morning. I have several clients who are in real estate deals and they all needed advice. Now. That took up most of my morning. A college student who was involved in a chain of convenience store robberies took up the rest. I'm not looking forward to defending him, but it's a paycheck.

The boring details of my morning get us to the restaurant. We each order cheeseburgers and iced tea. Then, before she busts at the seams, I tell Gina to tell me what she learned today.

"I talked to one of the paramedics on the scene," she starts. "He told me that when Bob Needham, the police chief, first got there he was talking about the investigation and how it would be the biggest investigation he'd ever been involved in and he wasn't looking forward to it. According to this paramedic, Needham said the reason he wanted to be a cop in a rural area like this is that there was less of a chance that he'd have to be involved in this kind of investigation."

"Anyway," she continues, "this conversation went on for quite some time while they were waiting for the coroner to arrive. The coroner gets there and, for a few more minutes, they're both talking about the investigation. Then, another cop comes in, whispers something in Needham's ear. Needham and the coroner go to another room."

"The paramedic didn't see Needham or the coroner the rest of the time he was there," she continues. "He said he was shocked when he read the paper and saw that Danny's death had been ruled a suicide."

"Obviously," I say, "Needham and the coroner went to talk to someone in another room … someone who told them to rule the death a suicide. Does the paramedic have any idea who was in the other room?"

"No," Gina says. "There was a police officer standing in the doorway Needham went through, kind of like he was guarding it."

"We should talk to the cop," I suggest.

"That's what I thought," Gina says. "But the paramedic told me he didn't know who the cop was. In all the confusion, he didn't think to ask. When he first saw in the paper that the death was a suicide, he thought the paper got it wrong somehow. He waited until the next day to see if there was a correction or explanation. When there wasn't, he started thinking about what happened at the scene. He tried to get a hold of the cop, but when he asked around, no one knew who he was talking about."

"Wow." I can't think of anything else to say.

"Yeah," she says. "There's even more than that, though. The paramedic testified in front of the grand jury. No one asked him anything. It was like ... You were there? Yes. You took the body away? Yes. You took it to the morgue? Yes. ... That was pretty much it."

"Unbelievable."

"It gets more and more unbelievable the more we learn," she says. "I think my next move is going back to Needham and asking him who told him to rule the death a suicide."

"Ask him just like that?"

"Sometimes the direct approach is the best way to go," she says. "I might catch him by surprise. Or, he might think I know more than I really do and spill his guts. I doubt I'll be that lucky, but you never know."

"Let's hope you're that lucky," I say. "Let's hope I'm that lucky when I'm checking out David Dwyer's business."

After we finish eating lunch, we both head back to work, agreeing that Gina will come to my house after work. We'll probably order pizza and down a few beers while discussing the new information we discovered today.

At any rate, I get to spend more time with Gina.

# Chapter Sixteen

The pizza was good. The beer is even better. Clapton on the stereo is always a plus. The conversation is going in a thousand different directions.

When Gina got in touch with Bob Needham all he said was that he had nothing to say, and my clients kept me hopping all day, so we really don't have anything to talk about on the Dwyer front.

It's a welcome change. As obsessed as I am with the whole Dwyer thing, I need a break. Now that I know I didn't kill Danny - I guess I believed that all along, but I needed Kevin Harper to confirm it - there's a huge load off my mind. But there is something still nagging at me, besides trying to find out who did kill Danny.

It's selfish, I know, but I can't help it. I'm afraid if people find out about my past, it will hurt my practice. It took me a long time to build up my practice after coming back to town after ten years. I slowly built it by defending people who had no idea who I was, not to mention that I charged less than any other lawyer in town. Slowly, very slowly, I built a reputation for being, if I do say so myself, a damn fine defense attorney. Eventually, even people who did know about my past started hiring me.

After a while, I even gained enough confidence to get involved in civic organizations. I'm proud that I've made a name for myself - a good name - and I don't need the Dwyer mess coming back to ruin all of that.

Anyone who really knew me back then - who knew all of us back then - knows I was outside of the drug scene and just looking in because of my friendship with Danny. We'd been friends since before either of us could walk, and I wasn't about to give up on him. Because I spent so much time around Danny and his new so-called friends, people who didn't know us thought I was part of the drug scene, too.

Bill Valentine and Judge Vaughn are obviously two of those people and I can't figure out why. They know I tried stopping Danny, tried getting him away from all of that. I'm from what Judge Vaughn considers a "good family," so I can't seem to get a handle on why he won't give me a break.

But at least the judge is easier on me than Valentine. He never misses an opportunity to remind me of the past. He's just playing a mind game with me now, but I know that if he could find a way to use it against me publicly he would.

"I think you just put your finger on it," Gina says, interrupting my rambling. "Maybe he's afraid you're going to run for D.A. and you'd kick his butt. If he keeps reminding you that you've got somewhat of a past, that puts the idea in your head that he'd bring it up during an election campaign."

"Who says I'm thinking of running for D.A.?" I ask, smiling, wondering how she read my mind, considering that's a thought that just slips in and out every so often.

"Wishful thinking," she says. "I think you'd make a great district attorney. You're ten times the lawyer Valentine is, and the other lawyers in his office can't even hold a candle to you."

"Flattery will get you everywhere," I say, smiling.

"This is more than flattery," she says. "I really believe you'd make an excellent district attorney."

"Why? Because I've already defended just about every criminal in the county?"

"No," she says. "You're a very talented lawyer. I think we need someone with your talent working for the good guys for a change. Besides, I think someone with your experience on the defense side would be beneficial for everyone. I think you'd be more likely to work with the defense to come to a fair conclusion for everyone."

"You think so, do you?"

"Yes, I do."

"I'll have to give that some thought Gina of *The Century*."

"I'm going to have to give some thought to going home," she

says. "It's getting pretty late."

"I kind of thought you'd spend the night here again."

"You did?," she asks, scrunching her nose.

"You make the idea of spending the sound so repulsive," I say, smiling.

"It's not at all," she says, laughing. "I just hadn't thought about it."

"Well, you did have three beers. I wouldn't want you to get picked up on a DUI."

"Oh please," she says. "That was hours ago."

"But still, we wouldn't want to push it," I say, raising my eyebrows.

"I suppose you're right," she says, winking. "I'll stay."

Gina and I walk out to her car so she can grab her backpack. When we get back inside the house, we head straight for Kathryn's room. I had a feeling this moment would be awkward, but I didn't think it would be this bad. I don't know how I can resist kissing her while she's gazing up at me with those big green eyes, but I can't seem to do it.

I think I'm afraid I'll be too clumsy. After all, it's been a while since I kissed a woman, and even then it was Vanessa so it doesn't really count anymore.

I'm going to have to forget the kiss. It's just not going to happen tonight, no matter how much her eyes are telling me she wants me to kiss her.

"I'll see you in the morning," I say, walking toward the door.

She smiles. "Thanks for a great day, Joe. I had fun."

"Me too."

"Night."

"Good night Gina of *The Century*."

For the first time in weeks Danny Dwyer isn't the foremost thought in my mind when my head hits the pillow.

\*\*\*\*\*\*\*\*\*\*

This is only the second day it's happened, but I like this new habit of planning my day with Gina over morning coffee. I could really get use to this. I especially like it since we probably won't get a chance to have lunch together today. She has an interview with Judge Vaughn and, for my own piece of mind, I have to start digging into David Dwyer's business.

Kathryn has a swim meet tonight. I invite Gina to go with me, not just because I want to be with her, but because Kathryn's been asking about her as well. Good sign. I think it would be fun for the three of us to go out for ice cream or something after the meet. I'm sure Vanessa wouldn't mind. Actually, Vanessa probably wouldn't even notice.

After Gina gets dressed, we walk out to her car together. I open the door and she tosses her purse and backpack inside then we stand there, awkwardly of course.

"So, do you want to just meet at the pool or ...?" she asks.

"Why don't we meet here first?" I say. "Then we can drive over together."

"I like that idea," she says, smiling.

"I was hoping you would."

"I'll see ya later then."

"You bet you will."

She starts getting into car, but I put my hand on her arm and she stands up again, facing me. I can't resist for another second and I give her a quick kiss on the lips. When I pull away, she's smiling. I'd say beaming, but that might be exaggerating a bit.

"Well," she says, letting out a little sigh. "I'll see ya later."

"You bet."

"We said all that before, didn't we?"

"I think we did."

"I gotta go," she says, shaking her head. "Wish I didn't."

"I wish you didn't, too."

"Have a great day, Joe."

"You too, Gina of *The Century*."

She gets into her car, fumbles with her keys, then starts the engine and pulls away, waving at me. Her smile is as big as mine feels.

# Chapter Seventeen

I'm surprised when my secretary tells me Gina's on the phone. As much as I miss her and want to talk to her, I have so much work today that I hate breaking away from it. At this rate, I'll never get to work on anything on the Dwyer front.

"I'm sorry to bother you," Gina says, "but I needed to talk to someone and you were the logical person."

"What's up?"

"I just got called into the office with Alex and Chris," she starts. "They told me they don't think it's appropriate for me to be spending so much time with you while I'm doing the Dwyer story."

"What?"

"That's what I said. But they said they think if I spend too much time with you it'll cloud my judgment."

"Cloud your judgment?"

"That's what I said. Then they said no one's sure about your involvement in the murder, so I shouldn't be spending so much time with you unless it's work related."

"They can't tell you that."

"That's what I said. But they said if it's effecting my job, they can tell me that."

"How do they think it's effecting your job?"

"They went back to that clouding my judgment argument. I told them I know this story better than anyone, and my spending time with you isn't clouding my judgment in any way. But then Chris said she covered the original story and she thinks she knows it better than I do and that I should be careful."

"Bullshit. Chris Palmer doesn't know shit," I say.

"I wish I could have said that to her, but I settled with something like trust me. I know what I'm doing."

"That works, too, I guess."

Gina laughs. "Thanks for making me laugh. But what am I going to do?"

"What do you want to do?"

"Ignore them."

"Then do it."

"But what if they find out I'm still hanging out with you? Actually, they think it's more than hanging out. They think I'm sleeping with you."

"What?"

"Apparently someone saw me leaving your house in the morning, so naturally we're sleeping together, right?"

"Small towns," I say. "Gotta love 'em."

Gina laughs again. "Back to the question. What am I going to do?"

"Do what feels right to you."

"What feels right is walking out of there and never looking back," she says. "But I don't want to do that while we're still working on the Dwyer story. It's a lot easier to get information as a reporter than it would be if I wasn't."

"So, let's get the story and get you outta there," I say.

"Let's hope it's that easy from now on," she says.

I wish I knew what to tell her, but I can't think of a thing. She's got to do what she thinks is best. I hope that doesn't mean we'll be spending less time together.

The best way for me to make sure she gets the story, I get peace of mind and she gets out of *The Century* is to get working on finding out all I can about David Dwyer's business. She told me one of her dreams is to win an Academy Award or Emmy Award for a screenplay. I'd like to help her get away from *The Century* so she can make her dream come true. If I can't let myself dream, the least I can do is help someone else's become a reality.

I'm happily surprised that the business office manager and new owner of the car dealership are very helpful.

It seems when Dwyer sold the business, he wanted to get out of there so fast he took hardly anything with him and the new owner saved it all. He said he thought Dwyer might change his mind about leaving everything, and he wanted to make sure it was all still there if he did. Even if he didn't, the new owner thought it might be able to be preserved for historical value. Dwyer's business was one of the oldest in the county, and historians are always looking for something for a new display or exhibit.

I'm not really in the mood to be around people, so I ask if I can take some things home with me. I gather up everything from the year Danny died as well as the two years before and two years after.

I go back to the office to make sure everything's still under control. After a brief stay there I head for home to change clothes and wait for Gina.

\*\*\*\*\*\*\*\*\*\*

I'm getting worried about Gina. She was supposed to be at my house half an hour ago. It's not like her not to call if she's going to be late. Actually, I don't know her well enough to know if it's like her or not, but I assume she's not the type of person to leave me hanging and wondering like this.

But here I am. Hanging and wondering. And worrying.

I keep looking at the clock, looking at the phone, looking at the clock. I promised Kathryn I'd be at the pool a little early to wish her luck. I know Kathryn will be disappointed if Gina's not with me, but if I don't leave soon I'll be late.

I don't want to call her cell phone because I'm afraid I'd interrupt an interview or something important, but at this point I don't have a choice. For my own peace of mind I have to call.

Now I'm even more worried. There's no answer.

As concerned as I am about Gina, I can't let Kathryn down. I call Gina's cell phone again and leave her a voice mail asking her to meet me at the pool.

# Chapter Eighteen

"Where's Kathryn?" Vanessa snaps at me just outside the door to the pool.

"What do mean where's Kathryn?" I ask. "She's supposed to be here."

"Exactly," she says in a surly tone. "If you're going to take care of her the least you can do is make sure she's at these things on time."

"Are you telling me Kathryn's not here?"

"You're a genius, Joe. No, Kathryn's not here. Where is she?"

"Vanessa, she lives with you. It's your job to know where she is."

"I can't know where she is every second of ..."

"She's eight years old. You're her mother. It's your job to know where she is every minute of the day! If she's not here ..."

"Are you saying you don't know where she is?" Vanessa asks.

"No I don't know," I say. "I assumed she'd be safe in her mother's care."

"I was only gone for a few minutes ..."

"What?"

"I was only gone for a few minutes," Vanessa said. "I had to run to the store and I thought she'd be fine while I was gone. When I got back and she wasn't there, I assumed you stopped by and brought her here."

"You thought I'd do that without leaving a note?" I ask. "And you never thought to call me?"

"You're not one of my favorite people to talk to anymore, Joe. I thought I'd just give you a piece of my mind once I got here."

"I wish you wouldn't give me a piece of your mind, Vanessa. You obviously don't have that much to spare."

Vanessa and I stop arguing long enough to call the police and report Kathryn missing. They listen to our story, take all the information they need, then tell us they'll issue an Amber Alert immediately.

We give the police our cell phone numbers in case they need to get a hold of us. Then we go to our separate homes to call all of Kathryn's friends to find out if they've seen her.

I'm so angry with Vanessa I can barely control it. I can't believe she lost Kathryn. Kathryn is responsible enough that she wouldn't leave the house without letting someone know. She'd also never miss a swim meet. She loves swimming and the thrill of competition.

First Gina. Now Kathryn. Something is terribly, terribly wrong here.

# Chapter Nineteen

All I can do is pace.

Kathryn's missing. Gina's missing. There's not a damn thing I can do about any of it. So, I pace.

I've been home for about an hour. I've called all of Kathryn's friends and anyone else I can think of. No one has seen her.

The phone rings. I race to it, hoping and praying it's Kathryn or someone who has heard from her.

It's Gina.

"Where are you?" I ask. "Are you okay? What's going on?"

"I hate to impose like this," she says, "but can you come and pick me up? I'm at the hospital."

"The hospital? Are you okay? Why are you at the hospital?"

"If you can come and get me, I'll explain everything after you get here."

I grab my car keys and cell phone, run out the door and race to the hospital. At this point I don't even care if I'm breaking speed limits. I need to get to Gina and find out what's happening.

I find her in an examining room talking to a police officer. Richie Banks was on the fringe of people Danny and I hung out with in high school. We knew each other pretty well, and liked each other well enough, but I wasn't as close to him as I was to other people in our group. Now, he's pretty much the only cop on the force I like so, if she's got to be talking to a cop, I'm glad it's him.

But why is she talking to a cop?

She tells me she'll explain everything after she gets home and into bed. She talked the doctor into not admitting her for observation and she wants to get out of the hospital before he changes his mind.

As we're walking to my car, Richie Banks asks about Kathryn.

"We haven't heard anything yet," I say. "If I could be any more worried, I would be."

"Kathryn's missing?" Gina asks.

"Yeah," I say. "No one's seen her for almost four hours. I'll explain all of that later."

"Good luck," Richie tells me. "If I hear anything I'll keep you posted."

I thank him then help Gina into my car.

"Is your car going to be okay here overnight?" I ask her.

"My car's not here," she says. "It's lying on its roof over a bank somewhere along Route 6."

"What?"

"I had an accid … Can I wait until I'm home in bed to tell you everything?"

"You can do whatever you want … except stay home by yourself tonight. You're staying at my house."

"I can't do that."

"Yes you can. I'm not taking no for an answer. I don't know what happened yet, but I know I don't want you spending the night alone. I'd spend the night with you at your house, but I need to be home in case Kathryn shows up or calls there."

"Tell me what's going on with Kathryn," she says.

The story of Kathryn disappearance gets us to Gina's house. She's as flabbergasted as I am that Vanessa could let this happen. I'm glad she feels that way because now I know I'm not overreacting.

At Gina's house I help her pack her favorite flannel nightshirt, a couple of changes of clothes and some personal items. We get back into my car then head for my house.

Inside, the first thing I do is check the answering machine. No messages.

With Kathryn missing, I don't feel right letting Gina sleep in her bedroom, so I get her settled in my room, after some protesting from her, I might add. She told me she couldn't take my bed. I told her I wouldn't have it any other way. End of argument.

I make her a cup of hot tea, then sit on the side of the bed while she tells me what happened. Another car forced her off the road, and she's sure it wasn't an accident.

"I don't know exactly how long the car had been following me," she says. "My mind was occupied with Judge Vaughn and the way the interview ended. It was strange. Actually, the interview was fine. Nothing out of the ordinary. He said everything you would expect a judge up for re-election to say.

"But it got kind of weird afterward. I've interviewed Judge Vaughn many times and one thing I learned about him is that he's not much for chitchat. But today he was working really hard at making idle conversation. That went on for about half an hour. Then, all of a sudden, he thanked me for coming all the way out to his house for the interview and showed me to the door.

"That's what I was thinking about when I was driving home. I know this is bad, but I wasn't paying much attention to the traffic or anything around me. Then, this car comes up behind me. It seems like it came from out of nowhere, but like I said, I wasn't really paying attention. Anyway, it races up behind me and hits my rear bumper."

"Are you serious?"

"Of course I'm serious," she says, sounding slightly annoyed.

"I didn't mean to doubt you," I say. "It's just that those things only happen in movies and suspense novels. You never hear about it happening to someone you actually know."

"Well, it happened to me," she says.

"I'm sorry I interrupted," I say. "Keep going."

"Okay. The car slows down, then speeds up and hits me again. Then it does it again. There's no place on that part of the road to pull over so I didn't know what to do. I thought about calling for help but I was afraid to take a hand off the wheel to get to my cell phone.

"So I sped up a little, hoping I could get to some place I could pull off the road. But then, you know that straight stretch just past the fork in the road? Well, when we got there, the other car pulls up beside me and starts hitting the side of my car. I don't know how many times it hit me before I lost control and my car went off the road and rolled down the bank."

"God Gina. I don't even know what to say."

"Neither do I. I guess I'm just thankful that I wasn't really hurt and I could get out of my car and crawl up the bank. I was only there for ten minutes or so before Richie Banks drove by in his patrol car."

"What did he say?" I ask.

"Not all that much, really. What could he say? But he was very nice. He drove me to the hospital, waited until the doctor examined me, then took a statement from me. It wasn't much of a statement though. The only thing I saw was a dark blue sedan. I don't even know what kind of car it was."

"I would think it shouldn't be that hard to find," I say. "It's got to have some pretty extensive damage."

"That's what Richie said," she tells me. "He said he's going to check with all the auto body and repair shops in the area and see what he can come up with."

"That's a start," I say.

Gina takes another sip of her tea.

"Joe, maybe I'm being paranoid," she says, "but do you think this could have any connection to Dwyer?"

"Maybe I'm a little paranoid, too, but I wouldn't be surprised."

"What about Kathryn's disappearance?" she asks. "Do you think that could be connected?"

"That was the furthest thing from my mind until I heard your story. Now, I think I shouldn't rule out that possibility."

"Do you think we should tell someone?" she asks.

"Like who? And what would we tell them?"

"We'd sound like lunatics if we said anything, wouldn't we?" she asks.

"Yeah. I'm afraid we would."

"So, what do we do?"

"I'm not sure yet. I'll have to think about ..."

The phone rings. I grab for it and pick it up even before it finishes the first ring.

"I pulled some strings for you," Richie Banks says. "This Amber

Alert thing is so new, and this is the first time we've had to issue one, I wanted to make sure we did it right. I made sure the chief sent press releases to the local media. So, all the radio stations should be running something about it now. And, it'll be in *The Century* in the morning."

"I don't know what to say. Thank you."

"No need to thank me," Richie says. "I wish I could do more, but it's about all we can do right now."

"Every little bit helps at this point."

"I know it's premature to be talking about this, and I don't want to alarm you unnecessarily," Richie says. "But is there any reason you can think of that someone would kidnap your daughter."

"No," I lie. My mind isn't functioning on a level where I could explain the Dwyer case to him.

"If you think of anything, or anything else that would help locate her, don't hesitate to give us a call."

"I won't."

"I know how most cops feel about defense attorneys ... and how you feel about most cops ... so if you'd feel more comfortable just calling me, do it," Richie says.

"Thank you. I will."

I hang up the phone then tell Gina what Richie said. After that, I try talking her into getting some sleep. I'm surprised the pain reliever she got at the hospital hasn't done that already.

"Too much adrenaline, I guess," she says.

"Well, Gina of *The Century*, you've got some pretty nasty bruises there, not to mention that broken wrist. That tells me that although you may not be feeling any pain right now, you're going to be one hurtin' lady soon. You're going to need some rest if you're going to heal faster."

"But I don't think I could sleep right now. You're not going to sleep. Can't I just do what you're doing?"

"Who says I'm not going to sleep?"

"I've seen you with Kathryn. I know how much you love and adore her. There's no way you're even going to be able to close your eyes, let alone sleep, until she's safe and sound."

"You're right. There's no way I could sleep."

"So, what are you going to do? Watch television? Bake cookies? Go on a mad cleaning spree? I'll help."

"Actually, I have some books and papers from David Dwyer's business here. I was thinking of going through those to see if I could find anything interesting."

"Perfect," she says. "I can help."

"I appreciate the offer, but I'd be much happier if you got some sleep. That's the best way you can help me right now."

She sighs.

"Joe, I have to tell you something. … I'm glad you offered to let me stay here tonight because I didn't want to be alone in my house. I don't want to be alone here either. I'm really scared."

I pull her close and hug her while she rests her head on my chest. She puts her arms around my waist and I stroke her hair.

"I'm sorry Gina. I should have realized you'd be scared. I wasn't thinking."

"I understand. Kathryn is your number one priority right now, and that's how it should be."

"But that doesn't take away from the fact that you're scared, and rightly so. I'll make a deal with you. If you promise to try and get some sleep, I'll sit on the bed right next to you while I'm looking through the Dwyer stuff."

"It's a deal," she says. She pulls away, looks at me with those big green eyes, then leans over and gently kisses my lips.

"Thanks Joe."

# Chapter Twenty

I guess I was more tired than I realized last night. Gina's soft breathing lulled me to sleep not long after I got into bed. I didn't even open one folder, one book, or one ledger from the Dwyer pile. I closed my eyes and that was it.

I know my sleep wasn't restful though. The nightmares about Danny have been replaced with one that's even worse: Kathryn wandering around aimlessly in the dark calling for me.

My heart is breaking because I don't know what to do. I don't know where to begin looking for her.

I hear a knock at the door and jump out of bed trying not to wake Gina.

"I wish I had some good news for you," Richie Banks says after I open the door, "but I'm afraid I don't. But I'm hoping I can talk to you for a few minutes about your daughter."

"You're not in uniform," I say, letting Richie inside the house. "Is this official business?"

"No. There's something that's been bothering me about your daughter's disappearance and I wanted to talk to you about it."

"Okay."

"Remember last night when I asked about the possibility that your daughter had been kidnapped?"

"Yes."

"The reason I asked is that a few guys down at the station brought up the possibility. Then when I ran it by you, you answered so quickly, without giving it a second thought, that it struck me as odd."

"What were the guys at the station saying?" I ask.

"It was all very cryptic. I didn't get a lot of it, just that they think it's a distinct possibility. Now, what do you think? Honestly."

"Before I answer that, let me ask you this," I say. "These guys who were talking about it, have they been on the force for a while or are they fairly new?"

"Old-timers," he said. "Three of them."

"Old-timers as in more than 20 years?"

"Yeah."

I sit at a chair at the dining room table and motion for Richie to do the same.

"You've got to promise me ... swear on your family's life ... that this doesn't go any further. Not yet anyway."

"I swear."

"Not only do I think Kathryn has been kidnapped, I think Gina's accident is related to this, too."

"Related to what?"

"Danny Dwyer."

"Danny Dwyer?"

"You're a good cop, Richie, so I have a feeling, somewhere in your mind, you know there's some kind of cover-up surrounding his murder."

"I've always thought so," he says.

"Well, Gina's doing an article for the paper on unsolved murders. Of course I didn't want it to run because of my involvement. There's a lot about that day I don't remember and, until very recently, I thought I might have been the one who killed Danny then blocked it out of my mind. I wanted everyone to forget the story, or at least forget I was connected."

"I can understand that," Richie says.

"I'm not going to bore you with all the details right now, but during the last few weeks Gina and I have both been doing some digging. We haven't uncovered much of anything yet, but I think we've gotten close enough to scare some people."

"But you don't know who it is who's scared?"

"Not yet. But we think we're getting closer. We know Needham, the former police chief, isn't telling Gina everything he knows. From the sound of things, I'd say there are a few more cops who know more than they're saying."

"You should tell someone about this," Richie says. "You should make it official so we can start an investigation."

"No one's done anything related to the Danny Dwyer case for more than 20 years. You think they'll do something now?"

"Good point. So, what do we now?"

"Just keep your eyes and ears open. I think that's all we can do right now. If either Gina or I find any kind of information pointing to anyone, we'll be sure to let you know."

"That's as good a plan as any at this point, I suppose."

# Chapter Twenty-one

Shortly after Richie walks out the door, Gina comes wandering into the living room, her eyes still half-closed.

"How long did I sleep?" she asks.

"Just a little longer than I did," I say. "How are you feeling?"

"Sore. Really sore. Any news about Kathryn?"

"Not news really. But Richie thinks she's been kidnapped."

"Why does he think that?"

I go over the entire conversation Richie and I had and she listens without interrupting once.

"Do you think he's on the up and up?"

"Totally," I say. "He may be the only honest cop left in the entire county. … Ya know, you don't look too good. Are you sure you're okay?"

"Getting more sore by the second, but other than that I'm fine."

"Why don't you take a pain reliever?"

"I'm not supposed to take it on an empty stomach."

"I can fix that."

I take Gina's hand and lead her to the kitchen. She sits at the table while I cook up some scrambled eggs and make some toast. While the food is cooking I pour her a glass of orange juice and watch her to make sure she drinks it.

We don't really talk during breakfast. There's not that much to say. We need to find something concrete to connect someone - anyone - to Danny's murder. That may be the only way to find Kathryn.

After breakfast, Gina says she thinks she might feel better if she takes a shower. While she's doing that, I call my office, tell Barbara I won't be in today and ask her to reschedule my appointments. Nothing is as important as finding Kathryn and making sure Gina stays safe.

While Gina's in the shower, I get a call from the police, who simply tell me they have nothing to tell me. I debate with myself on whether to mention the kidnapping theory. I'm not sure how seriously they'd consider the theory. Most of the cops on the department don't like me anyway, what with me keeping all those "criminals" out of jail and all, so I'm not sure how they'd react if they had to exert extra energy if Kathryn's disappearance turns out to be unrelated to the Dwyer case. I'd hope they could put their personal feelings aside and concentrate on a missing eight-year-old, but you never know.

It's the "you never know" that sways my decision not to tell the police about the kidnapping theory. I simply thank the officer who called and ask him to keep me informed.

After Gina gets out of the shower, I get her settled and comfortable on the couch. She refused to spend the day in bed, where I think she should be, but at least she'll be resting.

That was the plan anyway. Even on pain relievers that are supposed to make her drowsy she's wide-awake and insists on talking about the Dwyer case. I guess I'm relieved about that. At least I won't be obsessing alone.

We go over and over and over everything we know, and everything we need to know before we're going to solve this mystery. No new clues jump out at us. Nothing at all jumps out at us. After about an hour we figure all we can do is keep searching.

Another hour has gone by and, let me tell you, an hour goes by a lot slower when you look at the clock every two minutes. I offer to make Gina another cup of tea.

In the kitchen, I hear a strange knocking outside. It's not exactly on the back door but fairly close to it. I go to investigate.

Oh my God! It's Kathryn. As she looks up at me, I see in her tear-filled eyes fear, relief, love, hate, confusion all at the same time. There's a bandanna tied around her mouth. Her arms and ankles are bound with duct tape.

I remove the bandanna first. Kathryn bursts into tears but, understandably, doesn't say anything. She cries and cries and cries as I try to remove the duct tape without hurting her. I pick her up and carry her to the living room.

I sit on the couch, with Kathryn on my lap, next to a speechless Gina. I hold Kathryn tight and let her cry some more instead of asking questions. She'll talk when she's ready, I figure.

Gina says we should probably call the police and Vanessa to let them know Kathryn is here. She offers to make both calls. I let her because I don't want to let go of Kathryn yet.

She doesn't seem to be physically hurt, thank God. What she needs most right now, I assume, is to cry and be held. To tell you the truth, I could use a little of both right now myself.

I have no idea how much time has passed when Kathryn stopped crying and started talking.

"Daddy, I was so scared," she says, her face still buried in my chest. "It was so dark and cold."

"Do you know where you were?" I ask.

"No. The room was really big and really dark. The lights were off all the time. They brought me pizza one time, but didn't even turn on the lights then. They just put it right inside the door and told me to come and get it. I had to crawl on my hands and knees and feel around because I couldn't see. I couldn't eat anyway. I was too scared and my stomach hurt."

"So, you didn't see any people either?" I ask.

"No. Even when they brought me here I didn't see anybody. They had a thing over my eyes. When they took it off, they made me promise to keep my eyes closed until I heard their car pull away. They said if I opened my eyes they would know it and someone would have to pay for it."

"Kitty Kat, you keep saying 'they.' There was more than one person? Do you know how many?"

"Two people I think," she says.

"Would you recognize their voices if you heard them again?" I ask.

"I think so."

"Good girl," I say. "Do you have any idea how far away you

were?"

"Kind of," she says. "It kind of felt like it took us as long to get here today as it does when you drive me home from school."

"Good girl," I say again, hugging her tighter. "That's going to help a lot."

Actually, I'm not sure if it will help at all. We have nothing connecting Kathryn's kidnapping to the Dwyer case. No one has contacted us. We didn't get a ransom note or phone call. Nothing. I suppose it could have been a random kidnapping, a prank of some sort. But why?

Could it be related to Kathryn's swimming and have nothing whatsoever to do with the Dwyer case or me? What if some sick parent wants his daughter to be the best and knows Kathryn is standing in the way? Having her disappear on the night of a swim meet would be a good way for any of the other girls to get exposure, because right now all eyes are on Kathryn during every swim meet.

I suppose the best thing to do at the moment is keep asking Kathryn questions for as long as she'll let me and try gathering tidbits of information from her that I can eventually piece together.

Our reunion and question and answer session is interrupted by a knock at the door. Gina says she'll get it, but I tell her she should be resting. She insists on answering the door, saying I should keep holding Kathryn. I agree.

A few minutes later, Gina comes back in the living room with Richie Banks following her.

"This must be Kathryn," Richie says, smiling down at her.

Somehow, she forces a smile and says "Hi."

"I'm glad you're home safely," Richie says.

Kathryn smiles again.

"I hate to say this," Richie says, "but I've got to get a statement so we can wrap this up."

"I hate to say this," I say, "but I don't think wrapping it up is going to be that easy."

"No?" Richie asks.

I mouth the word "kidnapping." I'm sure Kathryn knows that's what happened to her, but I don't think she needs to hear the word out loud just yet.

"Kathryn," Richie says to my daughter, "I know you just got home and you want to be with your dad, but would you mind if I borrow him for a few minutes?"

"Where are you going?" Kathryn asks.

"Just into another room," Richie says. "I promise this won't take long."

Kathryn gives me a bear hug, then pulls away and nods her head. I pick her up off my lap and gently place her down on the couch next to Gina. I'm more than a little happy when Kathryn rests her head on Gina's shoulder and Gina drapes an arm around Kathryn.

Richie and I go to the kitchen to talk privately.

"I can't keep this under wraps forever," he says.

"I know, I know," I say. "But if we could just hold off on it for a little while ... a day or two maybe. I don't think it would be a good idea for this to hit the papers yet."

"I'll see what I can do," Richie says. "It was hard enough keeping all the details of Gina's accident out of the paper."

"I know it must have been," I say, "and don't think we don't appreciate it. But we really don't need word of this to get around yet. You know as well as I do that the more people who know there's an investigation, the harder it is to keep going."

"I know," Richie says. "Believe me, I know. You'll get dozens and dozens of false leads while the people involved in the crime find ways to remove themselves from it."

"After more than 20 years we're finally getting somewhere with the Dwyer case," I say. "I don't want to give the people involved any reason to go back into hiding."

"I can see that," Richie says. "I don't know exactly what you've got ... yet ... and you probably don't even know what you have yet. But you've got somebody pretty scared. They're scared enough to start doing stupid things .... Kidnapping Kathryn. Gina's accident. They should start making big mistakes soon and that will make uncovering them that much easier."

"Messing with my daughter was a bigger mistake than they realize. God, I want to know who 'they' are!"

"You and me both," Richie says. "But we'll find out who's responsible for all of this ... and they'll pay."

"You keep saying 'we,'" I say. "That means you're going to help us?"

"I already know more than I should," Richie says. "I've already done more than I should have to help you. I'm in. I'll do whatever I can from my end."

"I can't tell you how much I appreciate this," I say. "It was one thing when I was helping Gina get a story so I could get some kind of closure. Now, they've hurt my daughter. That's another thing all together. No one hurts my daughter and gets away with it."

# Chapter Twenty-two

Kathryn decides she wants to take a bath then go to bed. I can't say as I blame her. If I'd been through what she had, I probably wouldn't want to do anything but sleep. Then again, the way events of my life seem to show up in the form of nightmares, sleep might be the last thing I'd want. I hope Kathryn doesn't have the same problem that's been plaguing me for more than 20 years.

Gina offers to help Kathryn with her bath. Kathryn hugs her and tells her she'd like that very much. I think Kathryn's ordeal is helping Gina to not concentrate so much on what happened to her. I also think having Gina around is helping Kathryn deal with everything. Sometimes only a woman's touch can help.

It would be nice for Kathryn if the woman's touch was her mother's, but Vanessa hasn't shown up yet. It's been hours since Gina called Vanessa to let her know Kathryn's here. She hasn't even called to say hello yet.

If it wasn't Vanessa, I'd be worried that something happened to her, that she's the next link in this chain of events. But something tells me that's not the case at all. I'm sure something more important came up. How anything or anyone could be more important than Kathryn, I'll never know, but I'm sure I'll get Vanessa's explanation eventually.

In a strange way, I feel bad for Vanessa. I can only imagine what Kathryn must be thinking about her mother right now, but it can't be good. Kathryn hasn't even asked about her mother. No questions as to whether we called, if she knows Kathryn's back, when she's going to be here. Nothing. Not a word. Not saying a word about her mother speaks volumes.

Kathryn's in bed now, with Gina sitting next to her stroking her hair, trying to help her get to sleep. Kathryn's eyes are closed. She looks like an innocent little angel. She's much too young to have had that innocence stolen from her.

I sit on the other side of the bed and kiss Kathryn on the cheek. She stirs and starts to open her eyes. I tell her to keep them closed and try to get some sleep. Only a few minutes later, she drifts into sleep. I hope the nightmares don't interrupt and disturb her.

Gina and I slowly get up from Kathryn's bed, trying our best not to wake her up, and tiptoe out of the room. We leave the door open so we can hear her better if she calls.

"You, young lady," I say to Gina after we're back in the living room, "need to get some rest now, too."

"But I'm not tired," Gina says.

"You need rest," I say. "You may not realize it right now, but you do."

"I guess you're right," she says, reluctantly. "But I want to help with Dwyer."

"The best way you can help right now," I say, "is to get some rest and come back at full strength."

"Oh, I'll be more than full strength," she says. "I want to find whoever is responsible for this and make sure they pay ... for everything."

"You and me both," I say. "You and me both."

"We'll do it," she says. "I know we will."

"I know we will, too," I say. "We make a pretty good team."

"Yes we do," she says.

I kiss her lips, then fluff her pillows and tell her lie down on the couch. After she does, I cover her up with an afghan, kiss her forehead and tell her to get some sleep.

She doesn't argue with me. In fact, she was sleeping just seconds after her head hit the pillow. Obviously she was much more tired than she realized. I'm glad I talked her into sleeping because I do need her at full strength to help me with the Dwyer case. If nothing else, I need someone to talk to about it.

I go into the dining room and start looking through the books, ledgers and whatnot from David Dwyer's car dealership. Part of me wants nothing more than to pore over every word, every number until I find some kind of answer. Another part of me wants nothing more than to nurture Kathryn and Gina - even if it's just watching them sleep.

I know the best way to help Kathryn and Gina right now is to find out who did this to them, so I start poring, searching.

I'm barely into it when I hear a knock at the door. I run to answer it before the knocking wakes up Kathryn and Gina.

"Where is she?" Vanessa says, pushing past me and coming into the house.

"Keep your voice down," I say. "She's sleeping. Where the hell have you been?"

"Showing a house," Vanessa says. "I couldn't break away."

"Your daughter who mysteriously disappeared had been found, and you couldn't break away?"

"It's a huge commission if I make this sale," she says. "The commission on this one sale will be more than you make in a year."

I shake my head. "I don't remember you being so driven by money, Vanessa."

"Being a single mother makes you look at things differently," she says.

"Single mother?" I say, laughing at her preposterous statement.

"The only thing that's changed since the divorce is that we live in different houses. If anything, it's been easier on you since the divorce. Whenever Kathryn's with me, you don't have to worry about a thing. You can even pretend you don't have a daughter if you want to."

"How dare you say that to me?"

"How dare you insinuate that you have anything in common with single mothers? Single mothers raise their children alone. You have your child's father doing just as much, if not more, than you do. And, as incompetent as they may be, you have a legion of baby-sitters helping you. Don't even begin to tell me how difficult this is for you. Besides, you wanted full custody, remember?"

"Of course I want full custody," Vanessa says. "I'm her mother."

"Well, start acting like one."

"I've had enough," she says. "I'm going to see Kathryn."

"She's sleeping," I say, blocking her from going past the entranceway. "She needs to rest."

"She needs her mother," Vanessa says.

"She needs a mother," I say. "She needs a mother who wouldn't leave her alone and allow something like this happen to her."

"That's not fair," Vanessa says.

"You didn't see her eyes this morning," I say. "You didn't see the fear in her eyes. You didn't see how disturbed she was. You witness the complete and utter terror you see in your daughter's eyes, try to imagine the trauma she experienced, then you tell me that's not fair."

"Terror? Trauma?" she says. "What are you talking about?"

I sigh heavily. I didn't want to get into this with Vanessa, especially not now, but now I have no choice but to tell her the truth. Part of anyway.

"Vanessa," I say. "Kathryn was kidnapped."

"I want to see my daughter," Vanessa says, pushing past me.

She stops in the living after seeing Gina sleeping on the couch.

"What's she doing here?"

"Sleeping, obviously," I say. "And I appreciate it if you didn't wake her up."

"Why, may I ask, is she sleeping here?"

"If you must know, she was in an accident and I didn't think it was a good idea for her to be alone. She needed someone to take care of her."

"Well aren't you the model nurturer these days," Vanessa says, sarcastically.

"Shut up, Vanessa."

Finally, after all these years, I found a way to leave her speechless. The direct approach. I wish I would have tried telling her to shut up years ago.

She glares at me while leaving the living room and walking toward Kathryn's bedroom.

"She looks so peaceful," Vanessa whispers to me after I catch up with her standing in the doorway to Kathryn's room. "How could something like this have happened to her? Why did it happen?"

"I'm sure we'll have answers soon," I say, determined not to let her know that I know more than I'm telling her. I've already told her more than I wanted to.

"What have the police said?" she asks.

"They're working on it," I lie. "We'll know something when they do."

"I don't understand," Vanessa says, shaking her head. "What possible reason could there be for someone to kidnap Kathryn?"

I shrug, figuring keeping my mouth shut is the best move at the moment. But I do pull her into the hallway away from Kathryn's doorway. I still don't want her to hear the word "kidnap" and Vanessa, insensitive creature that she is, doesn't seem to have a problem flinging that word around.

"You don't think it could be related to one of your incorrigible criminals, do you?"

"Vanessa, don't even go there."

"Well, you never know. Some of those people are pretty unsavory, you have to admit. I wouldn't be surprised if one of those delinquents you couldn't keep out of jail had something to do with this."

"Vanessa, I'm pretty sure none of my clients are behind this."

"How can you be sure? I think we should mention this to the police."

"If you've thought of it," I say, "I'm sure they have, too."

"I think we should make sure."

"I'll take care of it, Vanessa. I've got a pretty good rapport going with one of the cops."

"There's a cop who doesn't hate you?"

"Let's make a deal," I say. "Until we find out who kidnapped Kathryn, let's stop slamming each other. It's not helping anyone or anything and it's adding unnecessary stress to both of us."

"I suppose you're right," she says. "It's a deal. So, tell me about this cop."

I tell her the cop is Richie and that we've known each other since high school. I don't feel the need to go into any more detail than that. I'm most certainly not going to mention anything about Danny Dwyer to her. She's one of the last people in the world who can be trusted with a secret, especially one of my secrets.

Also, when she found out about the whole Danny Dwyer mess, she took every opportunity to throw it in my face, and still does. Not for the same reason Bill Valentine does - whatever that reason may be - but for her own personal reasons. She asks how I could possibly criticize her friends and her lifestyle when I have a such a sordid past. She asks how I can be so self-righteous about her occasional pot smoking when I have a history of it myself. It goes on and on and on. I don't need her, of all people, bringing that up again. Not now.

Besides, she's already reaching for ways to prove Kathryn's kidnapping is my fault. I don't need to give her more ammunition.

Because Kathryn's asleep so she can't talk to her, and because we called a truce so she can't slam me, Vanessa has no reason to stay. I promise I'll let Kathryn know she was there. I also promise to call her as soon as Kathryn wakes up so she can come by again. She just knows her daughter "must be aching for her mother."

Before she leaves, I make Vanessa promise not to tell a soul about the kidnapping. I tell her it could hinder the investigation and it's better if we keep it all quiet for now. I'm sure she won't be able to keep her super-size mouth shut, but it was worth a try to ask. I'm hoping that she at least won't tell anyone who matters.

I don't have the heart to tell her Kathryn hasn't even asked for her yet. Even if we hadn't called the truce, I don't think I'd be able to tell her that. For some reason, a scene from "Gone With the Wind" pops into my head.

It's the scene where Rhett and Scarlet's daughter has just had a nightmare while she's traveling with her father. As Rhett is comforting her, the little girl asks for her mother. Rhett supposes that even a bad mother is better than no mother at all.

Sadly, I think that Kathryn is at the point where she doesn't want a mother at all. Or maybe she wants one, just not the one she has.

After Vanessa leaves, I start poring over the Dwyer papers again.

One of these days, I think, I'll be able to go through this without any interruptions and I might actually find some useful information.

But it won't be today, I have a feeling.

I hear Kathryn stirring and get up to see if she needs anything.

"Hi Kitty Kat," I say, walking into her bedroom and seeing that her eyes are open. "How was your nap?"

"It was good," she says.

"Hey, guess what?" I say, trying to sound as upbeat as I can. "Your mom was here."

"Oh."

"She looked in on you but she thought you needed sleep so she didn't wake you."

"Okay."

"Would like to call her and let her know you're all right?"

"Maybe later," Kathryn says. "She's probably too busy anyway."

"I'm sure she'd never be too busy to talk to you," I say, remembering the truce.

"Yes she would be."

I walk over to Kathryn's bed, sit on the edge and start patting her knee.

"I'm sorry Kitty Kat. I wish there was something I could do."

"You could let me live here," she says, looking up at me with her big blue eyes that are clouded with the threat of tears.

"There's nothing in the world I want more," I say, "but it's not that easy. Judge Cleland said he thinks you should be with your mom. But I'm working on changing that."

"You are?" she asks, her eyes clearing up and started to show that familiar sparkle.

"I sure am. There's a custody hearing scheduled for next month and I'm going to try to get the judge to change his mind and let you spend more time with me."

"How much more time?"

"I'm trying for full custody ... that's what your mom has now and ..."

"That's what I want," she says. "I want you to have full custody.

I want to live with you."

"Well, that was easy enough," I say, smiling. "I was going to talk with you about this in a couple weeks. But I guess we have it all settled, don't we?"

"Do you think the judge will let me live with you?"

"I sure hope so," I say. "But it might help if you told him what you want. Would you mind talking to Judge Cleland?"

"Nope. I want to tell him I want to live with you."

I guess it's true. There always is a bright side, a silver lining to every cloud. If Kathryn hadn't been kidnapped, this custody talk may have been a lot more difficult. Kathryn's decision may have been more difficult. It took this to make her realize that she doesn't want to live with her mother and that she's prepared to tell it to the judge.

Still, I feel bad for her. I can't imagine what it must be like to know you're not the first priority in your mother's life. Now it's my job to show her she's the first priority in mine.

"Are you hungry Kitty Kat? Can I make you some lunch?"

"I'm a little bit hungry, I guess. But I don't know what I want to eat."

"How 'bout if I surprise you?"

"Okay."

"Do you want to eat here, or the kitchen or …?"

"Can I eat in the den and watch a movie?" she asks, perking up a bit.

"Sure," I say. "Gina's taking a nap in there so you'll have to be quiet. Is that okay with you? If not, I'm sure Gina wouldn't mind moving to …"

"No, it's okay Daddy. I like Gina. I think she's way cool."

"You do, huh?"

"Yeah. She's smart and funny and nice."

"Yes, she is."

"And she's pretty."

"You think?"

"Don't you?" Kathryn asks, looking up at me. The familiar sparkle in her eyes is starting to come back.

"Yes, I do."

"I knew it," she says. "Know what else I like about Gina?"

"No. What else do you like about Gina?"

"She doesn't talk to me like I'm a kid. Some grown-ups are weird. They think they have to talk in baby talk until kids are teen-agers. They're pretty dumb."

"I'll admit some adults are pretty dumb. I'm glad Gina isn't one of them."

"Me too," Kathryn says.

"Okay," I say, not quite ready to discuss my love life with my eight-year-old daughter. That is, if you can call it a love life at this point. "Let's get you settled in the den and I'll make lunch."

We find Gina stirring and only half asleep in the den. She says she would love to watch a movie with Kathryn, and she's up for a little lunch, too. Kathryn decides she'd like to rest on the couch with Gina. They arrange themselves with Gina's head on one side, Kathryn's on the other. They look very comfortable and cozy. It makes me smile.

I leave them watching "The Wizard of Oz" while I go to the kitchen to fix lunch. Kathryn's favorite lunch is crunchy peanut butter and banana on toast. I'm hoping Gina likes that, too, because that's what she's getting. Somehow, though, she's seems like a peanut butter and banana woman. She is an Elvis fan, after all.

While I'm waiting for the bread to toast I'm thinking about how relieved I am that I saw a little bit of spark in Kathryn. I was beginning to worry about her. She's always been able to bounce back quickly from any kind of tragedy and trauma.

I realize that it's only been a few hours since she's been home, but sometimes it only takes her a few hours before she's back to her old self.

For instance, when Vanessa's mother died two years ago Kathryn was the one keeping all her cousins - and even some aunts and uncles for that matter - from breaking down.

Last year, Kathryn's best friend and her family were killed in a car accident. Again, Kathryn was the person who tried keeping everyone strong.

Even with the divorce she was a real trooper. Of course she was upset, but she tried her best to keep me looking on the bright side. Among other things, she said her mother and I wouldn't be fighting as much so the time we spent together would be quality time.

Of course she was right in regard to the time she and I spend together. Obviously, it's not true in regard to Vanessa. I'm sure Vanessa doesn't realize how much she's hurting Kathryn. I'm sure some part of her might care that she's hurting Kathryn, if she opened her eyes enough to see it. But ultimately she's only hurting herself. One day she's going to wake up and realize she missed out on spending time with a great kid.

But that's her problem.

Despite that, I give her a call to let her know Kathryn's awake. Of course I get her voice mail. It's anyone's guess as to when or if she'll return the call or show up here.

After putting the sandwiches together and putting a handful of potato chips on each plate, I carry them to the den and place them on the coffee table. I was right. Gina is a peanut butter and banana woman.

They're at the part of the movie where Dorothy has just arrived in Munchkinland. Gina is just as into the movie as Kathryn is. I'm amazed every time I watch this movie with Kathryn because she's so wide-eyed it's almost as if she's never seen it before. The only thing that gives her away is that she knows every line of dialog and every song lyric. Gina is watching the movie with the same wide-eyed wonder - she's singing along, too. I can't help but smile.

The smiling ends shortly after Dorothy, the Scarecrow and the Tin Man meet the Cowardly Lion. That's when the doorbell rings and the Wicked Witch, uh, sorry, Vanessa returns.

"Oh honey!" Vanessa says, making her grand entrance into the den. She kneels on the floor in front of Kathryn and hugs her tight. Kathryn picks up the remote control and puts the movie on pause. "Are you okay? Are you hurt?"

"I'm fine," Kathryn says.

Vanessa pulls away and looks Kathryn up and down. "You look

okay," she says. "Are you sure there's nothing wrong?"

"I'm fine Mom."

"Well, I see you've eaten lunch," Vanessa says. "Why don't we get you dressed and get you home."

"I want to stay here."

Unbelievably enough, Vanessa looks taken aback and, could it be? Hurt?

"Well, honey," Vanessa says, "wouldn't you like to be home in your own room in your own bed?"

"I have a room and a bed here."

Vanessa looks at me. I shrug. I have no intention of helping her get out of this one. I want Kathryn with me. It's what I've always wanted. There's no way I'm going to make Kathryn go home with her mother if she doesn't want to go.

Vanessa makes a motion with her head toward the living room. We both stand up and head that way.

"I really think the best thing for her is to be home," Vanessa says.

"I think the best thing for her is what she wants to do," I say.

"Of course you'd say that," she says.

"I refuse to fight about this Vanessa. Kathryn wants to be here. If you care about her at all you'll leave without causing a scene."

She glares at me and stomps back to the den.

"Kathryn honey," Vanessa says, "Are you sure you wouldn't rather be home?"

"I'm sure Mom. Besides, Daddy can take time off from work and be with me. You can't."

I want to high-five Kathryn and shout "You go girl!" but I keep all that inside.

Vanessa is dumbfounded. She kneels down in front of Kathryn again and hugs her.

"You promise you'll call me if you need anything," Vanessa says.

"Sure Mom."

Vanessa stands up and starts walking toward the front door without even telling Kathryn she loves her. She turns around to see if I'm following her. When she sees that I'm not, she makes that annoying head motion again.

Standing in the doorway, she asks how long "that reporter" intends on staying at my house.

"I didn't think you noticed Gina was here," I say. "You didn't acknowledge her."

"Just answer the question, Joe."

"Gina will be here as long as we think it's necessary."

"Do you think having her here is the best thing for Kathryn right now?"

"Don't even go there, Vanessa," I say, my temper starting to rise.

"Personally, I think it's vital right now for Kathryn to know how important she is to us. I don't think having that woman in your home is sending the right message."

"First of all, if you bothered to ever talk to your daughter, you would know that she thinks the world of Gina. She enjoys spending time with her and, before you got here, they were having fun watching 'The Wizard of Oz.' Second," I say, doing my best to keep my anger in check, "I'd hate to remind you of the reason our marriage ended. But I will say that you're the last person in the world who should be talking about sending the wrong message to Kathryn."

I guess Vanessa got the point. She stormed from the house to car, gunned her engine and sped down the street. I hope I don't have to deal with her for a while - at least for the rest of the day. I'd just like to spend time with Kathryn and Gina.

And the Dwyer books.

# Chapter Twenty-three

I tell Richie Banks that Kathryn hasn't really said much at all about the kidnapping. I figure she'll talk about it when she's ready. Richie says that's probably true, but he'd like to ask her a few questions anyway.

He tells me he's decided to work on the investigation during his off duty hours as a favor to me. I find that a bit odd because we aren't really friends, and never were, but if it's going to help solve the Dwyer case and lead me to the kidnappers, I'm not going to question him.

As for his questioning Kathryn, he's going to have to wait a while. Right after the movie she and Gina went back to sleep, which is where they are right now - and looking awfully cute together, I might add. I think sleep is the best thing for them and tell Richie I'd rather not wake up either of them. Richie agrees that they probably both need sleep. He asks if it would be all right if he waited here for Kathryn to wake up.

I tell him I don't mind if he stays, but I'm thinking that that's just one more thing keeping me from looking through the Dwyer books. The more I'm kept from looking at them, the more I'm drawn to them. I have no idea what's in them, but with each interruption I'm surer there's something. I don't think fate or karma or whatever higher power is surrounding this case would let me go to all this trouble for nothing.

While we're waiting for Kathryn to wake up, Richie and I take the time to get to know each other better. At least that's the way the conversation started. It didn't take long for us to get back to Danny Dwyer.

Richie reminds me of an incident during our freshman year of high school when a group of senior jocks was teasing him mercilessly about being a "band geek." While most of the kids who walked by either laughed, joined in on the teasing or ignored it all, Danny and I stepped in and stood up for Richie. Because the jocks knew and respected my older brother who had graduated a year earlier, not to mention the fact everyone knew who Danny's father was, they stopped teasing Richie, albeit reluctantly, and not without getting a few shots in at me and Danny.

I remembered the incident, but I didn't remember Richie was the kid we stood up for. Richie said that's probably because he quit band that day and started concentrating on sports. He said good-bye to the band geek, and didn't look back until years later. It was Danny who helped him look back.

Richie's girlfriend lived next door to Danny, so Richie was able to see what was happening to Danny. In the beginning, Danny had coherent moments when he and Richie talked. The talks came about during calls to the police about loud parties or disturbances at Danny's house. When Danny came outside to talk to the police, Richie would try to help. He tried talking some sense into Danny - much like I did - but his efforts were in vain, too. Obviously.

Richie says the reason he wants to help me solve this case is that he feels he didn't do enough to help Danny when he was alive. The least he can do is try to help put some closure to this.

To quote Rob Lowe in "St. Elmo's Fire," I'm in touch with that emotion.

I was so into the conversation with Richie that I'd almost forgotten he was here to talk with Kathryn. It was Gina coming into the dining room that reminded me. She and Kathryn had both woken up from their naps and wanted some apple juice. I tell Gina to go back to the den and lie down. I'll get the juice and be right in. After I pour two glasses of juice, Richie and I head for the den.

I tell Kathryn why Richie's here and ask her if she's up to answering a few questions. Despite the hint of trepidation in her voice, she says she's ready to answer questions, but she doesn't think she'll be much help.

"I'm sure you'll be a great help," Richie says. "I just want you to start at the beginning and tell me everything that happened."

"Okay," she says. "I'll try to remember everything."

I'm not sure I want to hear this. I already hate these guys. Hearing everything they did to my daughter is certain to make me hate them even more.

As soon as Kathryn starts talking, Gina drapes her arm around Kathryn's shoulders. Kathryn leans closer to Gina, resting her head on Gina's shoulder.

Kathryn starts the tale of her ordeal. Vanessa told her she had to go out for a few minutes, but when she got back she'd be ready to go to the swim meet. Vanessa asked if Kathryn would be all right by herself. Kathryn nodded and started filling her backpack with everything she needed. She said she heard noise in another part of the house, but assumed her mother forgot something and came back to get it. She didn't give it a second thought.

Next thing she knew, two men wearing black clothes and black ski masks burst into her bedroom and told her not to say a word. They tied a bandanna around her mouth, then another around her eyes. They taped her ankles together, then her wrists, then one of them picked her up, carried her out of the house and dropped in the back seat of a car.

After driving for "just a little while" with no one saying a word, the car stopped. One of the men picked her up again and carried her to a "big, dark room." That's where she stayed for hours. She said she didn't know how many hours it was until she got home. In the big, dark room, they told her they would take the tape, gag and blindfold off her if she promised to stay in the spot they put her in and not move an inch. She promised.

They left her with a bottle of water to drink. Every so often, one of them would stand outside the door and ask if she needed to use the restroom. When she did, they told her to keep her closed, they came in, held her hand and lead her a few feet from where she was to the restroom. When she finished, they took her hand again and lead her back to her spot near the door.

Once, they brought her pizza and sat in the room while she ate a slice. She told us her stomach hurt so badly that she didn't want to eat, but she knew she better eat something because she didn't know when they'd bring her something else.

After she ate, they told her she should try to get some sleep. She knew she wouldn't be able to, but didn't say anything to them about it. Instead, she just sat on the cold floor with her back against the wall and her knees pulled to her chest.

She said she wanted to cry, but she didn't want the men to know she was that scared. She was mad, too, that one of the men stayed in the room with her all night. She wanted him to leave so she could cry without anyone seeing her.

As she said, she had no way of telling time so she didn't know how much time had passed when the other man came back into the room. Without saying a word, they gagged and blindfolded her again, then re-taped her ankles and wrists. One of them carried her to the car and dropped her in the back seat again.

After stopping the car, but leaving the engine running, one of them carried her to, what she would later see was, the back porch of my house. He told her he was going to take the blindfold off, but if she knew what was good for she would keep her eyes closed until she heard the car pull away.

After she heard the car pull away, she opened her eyes and was "real, real happy" to see that she was at my house. She started kicking the door until I heard her.

I'm very proud of her. She didn't cry at all during the entire telling of her story. I get up and give her a hug. She hugs me back. Tight.

Gina's cell phone had rung while Kathryn was telling her story, but Gina decided not to answer it. She figured Kathryn needed her more than whoever was calling did. But now, she decides she should probably go see if whoever it was left her voice mail. She goes to the dining room where her phone is.

"You did great," Richie tells Kathryn. "You did so great, as a matter of fact, that I don't have all that many questions. Are you still up to answering them?"

Kathryn nods.

"Great," Richie says, smiling at her. "You said you were in the car for just a little a while. Do you have any idea how many minutes it was?"

"I don't really know how many minutes," Kathryn says, "but it felt like about the same time as it takes Daddy to drive me from here to school."

"Great," Richie says. "That's a big help. Do you remember any sounds while you were driving? Kids playing? Lots of traffic in one particular area? Anything?"

"The windows were closed except for one time. I think one of the men threw a cigarette out the window because after he closed the window I didn't smell smoke anymore," Kathryn says. "Anyway, I didn't hear very much."

"You're very observant to have noticed the window and the cigarette," Richie says. "Did you notice anything else?"

"Ummm ... I felt the car go over railroad tracks. Twice. Oh yeah," she says, seeming a bit excited that she's remembering things. "When the window was opened I smelled the oil refinery. It stunk really bad. That room we were in stunk bad, too. And the restroom was yucky."

"You're such a big help," Richie says. "Anything else you remember?"

"Well, while we were in the car, I could see a little bit under the blindfold. The carpet and the seats in the car were dark blue."

"That's great Kathryn," Richie says. "You're doing great!"

"I don't really remember anything else," Kathryn says. "I'm sorry."

"Don't be sorry," Richie tells her. "You remembered more than a lot of grown-ups would have if they'd been in your position."

"Really?" she asks, with a tone of pride her in voice.

"Really," Richie says. "I'm very proud of you."

"Me too, Kitty Kat," I say, hugging her tight.

"Gina," Richie says while my daughter and I are hugging each other. "I didn't see you standing there."

"I didn't want to interrupt," Gina says, standing in the doorway.

"What's wrong, Gina?" I ask, slowly breaking away from Kathryn as I see the distressed look on Gina's face.

"I'm not sure I should say this in front of Kathryn," Gina says, "but since we're all in this together I guess she should know what's happening."

"What's wrong?" I ask again.

She punches a few numbers into her cell phone, then hands the phone to me. The message on her voice mail says "That was a warning. Next time you won't be so lucky."

"Richie needs to hear this," I say, handing the phone back to Gina. She punches the numbers in again then hands the phone to Richie.

"Kathryn," Richie says after handing the phone back to Gina. "You need to hear this, too. I don't want you to be afraid of what the man is saying because we're going to protect you. I just want you listen carefully and tell me if you recognize his voice."

Gina punches in the numbers one more time then hands the phone to Kathryn.

"I think that's one of them," Kathryn says, handing the phone to Gina. "But I'm not really sure. They didn't talk too much."

"Good enough," Richie says. "Gina, I'd like to take your phone so I can tape a copy of that message. Will that be a problem for you?"

"Not having my cell phone won't be a problem," Gina says. "My car being forced off the road is a problem. Do what you have to do."

"Well," Richie says. "I think I've got a good start here. Now I have to start putting it all together."

"I can't tell you how much I appreciate this," I say.

We all jump a bit when the phone rings. Richie tells me to let the machine get it. He says maybe he's spooked after hearing the message on Gina's voice mail or maybe it's wishful thinking, but if it's the "perps" he wants it on tape.

Or maybe he's psychic.

The same voice we had all just heard on Gina's voice mail left a similar message on my answering machine.

"That was just a warning," the voice said. "Next time your daughter won't be so lucky."

All the blood rushes from Kathryn's face. She's pale as a ghost.

I hug her, trying to comfort her and let her know everything's going to be all right.

I wish I believed that.

# Chapter Twenty-four

Not surprisingly, Vanessa hasn't called even once since she left my house earlier today. She knows - or at least she should know - it's Kathryn's bedtime. You would think she'd call to say goodnight.

Not hearing from her mother, however, didn't seem to keep Kathryn from falling asleep. As soon as her head hit the pillow, she was out. I was sure all the excitement, if that's what it can be called, would have kept her awake. I'm glad it didn't.

Gina and I are sitting in the dining room talking while I'm finally looking through the Dwyer books. I don't know what I expected to find, but so far they're as dry as dirt.

"You have good instincts," Gina tells me. "I'm sure you're right about this. There's got to be something there and I'm confident you'll find it."

"That's what your good instincts are telling you?" I ask, still looking through one of the dozens of ledger books.

"Yes," she says. "And I can't quite put my finger on it, but my instincts are telling me something's up with Judge Vaughn."

"You think Judge Vaughn is involved in this?" I ask, looking up from the ledger books.

"I didn't say that. But he was acting really strange right after the interview. We've chatted before, but I've never considered him overly chatty. But the other day I couldn't shut him up. Then, all of a sudden, he stopped talking and sent me on my way. It was almost as if he was told to keep me there until a certain time." She stops, then starts laughing. "Geez. Am I being paranoid now or what?"

"Maybe," I say. "Maybe not. You never know."

"Oh please," she says. "You think Judge Vaughn, Judge Warren Vaughn, the paragon of truth, justice and the American way in

Brafferd County has some connection with me being run off the road and Kathryn's kidnapping?"

"Judging by the sarcasm dripping from your lips, I'd say you don't think as highly of Judge Vaughn as most people in the county do," I say.

"I'm not one of his biggest fans," she says. "Let's just put it that way."

"Why not?"

"I don't know. It's just a feeling."

"Come on now," I say. "It has to be more than that. What is your feeling based on?"

"Good families," she says. "It's the way he treats people from what he perceives as good families. If these people come from such good families, shouldn't the families take care of their own and set them on the straight and narrow path before they get in so deep that they end up in his courtroom? Isn't it the people who come from bad families who should be getting a break? They're the ones who don't know any better and have to be taught how to be a productive member of society."

"I agree with most of what you said," I tell her. "But it's not always that easy to set someone on the straight and narrow path."

"I'm sorry," she says. "I know you tried with Danny. But think about this. What if everything with Danny was going on today? How would you feel if he'd been dragged into court over and over and Judge Vaughn kept sending him to rehab or putting him on house arrest because he came from a good family?"

"I'd be pissed," I say.

"Exactly. I don't know if jail time would help these people any more than what he's doing, but at least it would be fair. ... Joe," she says as I'm staring at the ceiling. "What are you thinking?"

"I'm thinking about how Danny was never arrested," I say. "All the times the police were called to his house and he was never arrested. Anyone who walked into that house, even just a few steps into the house, would know there were drugs there. Hell, sometimes there were syringes, pills and bongs on the coffee table."

"Any theories on why he was never arrested?" Gina asks.

"Other than the good family thing? No. But I'm working on it."

I turn a page of the ledger book and something catches my eye. Finally. In one month, four $5,000 checks were recorded as being sent to WV Quality Cars. That's one check a week. Twenty thousand dollars a month. I turn the page. Another $20,000. I turn another page. Another $20,000.

"What is it?" Gina asks. "What did you find?"

"I'm not exactly sure yet," I say, still flipping pages and finding more money being sent to WV Quality Cars. "But I know it's time to talk to Kevin Harper again."

# Chapter Twenty-five

"I can take a few personal days," Richie tells me. "It's really no problem."

"I can't ask you to use your personal days for me," I say.

"Number one, you're not asking me. I'm offering," he says. "Number two, I want to do it ... for Danny."

"If you insist," I say.

"I do. Besides, it's a nice drive. The West Virginia mountains are awesome."

I would have felt more comfortable with Richie staying here to look in on Kathryn and Gina, but I'm glad I'll have company on the trip. Now, I just have to figure out what to do about Kathryn and Gina. They both insist they're fine and perfectly able to take care of each other. But I can't help but worry. It's what I've been doing best lately.

The thing I'm most worried about is Vanessa's reaction when she finds out I've left Kathryn in Gina's care. Then again, all I would have to do if Vanessa starts in on that is mention her not-so-stellar choices in baby-sitters for Kathryn. At least Gina is a responsible adult. And she cares about Kathryn. That's more than I can say for any of the teen-age bimbos Vanessa has had watching Kathryn.

I hope Gina's up to this. She's still sore and a little a weak from the accident, although she's trying to pretend she's back to 100 percent. But, she and Kathryn did say they'd take care of each other, so that tells me Kathryn won't be asking too much of Gina. They said they'd probably order pizza and watch movies for the two days I'm planning on being away. They'll probably have a blast.

\*\*\*\*\*\*\*\*\*\*\*

Richie and I just drove past a WV Quality Cars lot and the butterflies immediately started stirring in my stomach. We're getting closer to Kevin Harper and, with any luck, some answers.

My cell phone rings and, when I see that the call is coming from my home phone, my stomach gets even jitterier. Something must be wrong.

"There's nothing wrong," Gina says as soon as I answer. "I knew that's what you'd be thinking."

"You think you know me pretty well, don't you?" I ask.

"Yeah, I think I do," she says. "But that's beside the point. This may sound crazy, but I have a hunch. Did you ever find out who owns WV Quality Cars?"

"Not yet," I say. "Richie was going to do that while I talked to Kevin."

"I think it would be a good idea to find out who owns it before you talk to Kevin," she says. "Like I said, this is just a hunch, but I think Judge Vaughn is involved in all of this. I've been thinking about this for an hour or so, then it hit me. WV Quality Cars. WV. Warren Vaughn. Judge Warren Vaughn."

"You're right," I say. "It does sound crazy. What make you think about that? What's your hunch based on?"

"The judge stopped by the house this morning to pay you a visit," she says. "It was just odd. The whole thing was odd."

"Odd how?" I ask.

"Odd how? Does the judge normally stop by to visit you?"

"Well, no. What did he say? What was the reason for stopping by?"

"He said he heard about Kathryn's ordeal and my accident and wanted to see how we were all holding up."

"How did he hear about Kathryn?"

"That's what I asked him," she says. "He just said 'Word gets around.' I suppose that's an innocent enough answer. I mean, cops do talk and so do other people, and then there was the Amber Alert.

I suppose enough people knew and the word could have just gotten around to him. But it just seems strange."

"You're right. That does seem strange. Let's say that is what happened. Why couldn't he have just called and asked me about Kathryn."

"Exactly," Gina says. "Also, he said he heard about my accident. Fine, but how did he know I was here? He didn't say one word about being surprised to see me here or not having to stop by my house to check on me. Nothing like that. It's as if he expected me to be here."

"Did you ask him about that?"

"No," she says. "I didn't even think about that part of it until after he left and I started rerunning the conversation in my head."

"Okay. Well, what else did he say?"

"Not much really. I did take notes, though, when I started thinking about it again after he left."

"Always the reporter," I say, smiling.

"Yep," she says, laughing. "Comes in handy sometimes. And, let me tell you. Taking notes wasn't easy with a broken wrist. But, while I was taking notes, I remembered something Chris told me when I started working on the story. She said she thought Judge Vaughn knew more than he was saying. She even made me write 'WV' in my notes so I wouldn't forget to check it out. Unfortunately, until now, I hadn't gotten far enough to link him to anything, so I didn't have anything to ask him. Anyway, I'd feel a lot better if you checked that out before you talk to Kevin. If the judge is involved somehow, you need to know that before you talk to Kevin as well."

"You're right. We'll check it out," I say, remembering that I had stolen Gina's notebook and copied it. I feel even more guilty about that now than ever. "We were planning on taking the easy way out and just asking someone at the dealership who owns the place. But now, I think it would be better if we stopped at the county records office."

"I think so, too," she says. "We don't know how WV fits into Danny's murder, if it does at all. But if the judge is involved in all of this, you can't give anyone the even the slightest idea that you know."

"Right," I say. "Did you tell the judge where I am or what I'm doing?"

"I just told him you were working on a case. He didn't push it."

"Okay. That works."

Before ending the call, Gina tells me she and Kathryn are doing just fine and I have no reason to worry. They've been watching movies, talking and having a wonderful time getting to know each other.

Normally, I'd say that's one less thing to worry about. But this time, I can't stop worrying no matter what I do.

Richie is incredulous when I tell him about Gina's theory on the judge. But then he says anything's possible. He says the judge seems like a great guy, but you can't always judge a book by its cover.

That cliché makes me think of Gina. It seems like years ago that she told me she's trying to cut down on her use of clichés. It's hard to believe it's been less than a month and that so much has happened during that time.

Before going to WV Quality Cars, Richie and I stop at the county records office to find out who owns the business. We're directed to a bank of computers designated for public use. We find more than we bargained for.

# Chapter Twenty-six

Judge Warren Vaughn is, in fact an owner of WV Quality Cars. His partner is William Valentine.

With that bit of information in hand, Richie and I decide we have to do a little more digging before confronting Kevin again. It's totally possible now, we believe, that Kevin knows much more than he's saying. We need as much information as we can possibly dig up before we even think about setting foot in the WV office again.

We figure that we have to find out how far back the Judge Vaughn/ Bill Valentine connection goes. While we're at it, we decide finding out as much about Kevin Harper as we can would be beneficial as well.

Again, we discover more than we bargained for. In looking up birth records and other records, we learn that Kevin Harper is Bill Valentine's grandson.

My first reaction is anger. How dare that bastard throw the Danny Dwyer situation in my face all these years when his own grandson was one of the people supplying Danny with the drugs?

Although that question will probably never be answered, other questions are being answered for me as everything gets clearer - and murkier at the same time.

Now I know why Kevin was never arrested. Everyone in law enforcement knew he was one of the main suppliers, but nothing was ever done about it. He did pretty much whatever he wanted to do, wherever he wanted to do it.

The question in all of this is: Why wasn't it common knowledge that Kevin is Bill Valentine's grandson?

There's just too much information coming at us too fast now. Richie and I are having a hard time digesting it all, but we're still hungry for more so we keep digging. I take a break long enough to call Gina and tell her not to answer the door for anyone.

"What's wrong?" she asks.

"You were right about Judge Vaughn," I say. "I can't get into everything else right now. We have to finish up here before the office closes, then we want to get to the library before it closes, so we don't have a lot of time. Just promise me to keep the doors locked and don't open them for anyone."

"I promise," she says. "Be careful."

"I will. You be careful, too, and keep an even closer eye on Kathryn."

If ever I wished I could be three or four places at once, it's now.

I need to be here. I need to be working with my clients. Most important, I need to be with Kathryn and Gina. Lounging on a beach in Bermuda would be nice, too.

But since I obviously don't possess the magical powers I would need to be in more than one place, I have to make the most of my time here and hope everything else takes care of itself.

By the time Richie and I finish all the research we needed to do, the car dealership is closed. We opt not to go to Kevin's house to talk to him. Being in a public place would be much safer.

We also decide spending the night in Elkins is not a wise move. We don't want Kevin to get wind of the fact that we're here. So, we drive to the next town that has a motel and restaurant and decide to spend the night there.

Over dinner we discuss what we've got so far.

We know Danny Dwyer is dead. We know he used drugs, but we don't know if that's related to his death. We know Kevin Harper supplied the drugs. We know Kevin Harper is the grandson of Bill Valentine, the district attorney who gave up on trying to find Danny's killer. We know Bill Valentine and Judge Warren Vaughn own WV Quality Cars. We know Danny's father David Dwyer, by way of his troubled business, sent $20,000 a month to WV Quality Cars beginning about a year before Danny died.

What we don't know - yet - is how the pieces of this puzzle fit.

Add to that puzzle the fact that when Gina and I started working on this case together, Gina's car was run off the road and my daughter was kidnapped. Unrelated events? Possible, but not probable.

Richie and I spend the next hour or so bouncing ideas off each other, but none of them seem to be realistic. We decide that's because we can't quite figure out how Judge Vaughn fits into the picture. We learned through our research at the library that he and Bill Valentine have been lifelong friends, as had their fathers. They went to school together from grade school to college to law school. After graduating from law school, their fathers retired and turned WV Quality Cars over to their sons. While Valentine and Vaughn still own the business, they turned the everyday operation over to relatives so they could pursue their law careers.

Vaughn was the first to arrive in Brafferd County, Pennsylvania. After two years of working with an established law firm, he opened his own practice. Valentine joined him shortly after that. Ten years later, in the same election, Vaughn was elected judge and Valentine was elected district attorney. They've held the positions ever since.

Since their arrival in Brafferd County nearly 40 years ago, they've become pillars of society. They both currently serve on the board of directors of the medical center, the university, the children's home, the local unit of the American Cancer Society and the United Way. They're both members of the Kiwanis and Rotary clubs, among other organizations and charitable groups.

How could anyone think there's anything shady in their past?

It's hard. It's very hard. But Richie and I know there's a connection between them and Danny's murder. We feel it in our bones.

We know we'll fit the puzzle pieces together soon.

# Chapter Twenty-seven

It's a good thing we did all the research we did yesterday or the trip would have been a bust. When we arrived at WV this morning, we found out that Kevin Harper is out of town on a two-week vacation. No one knows where he is.

I think about calling Gina to let her and Kathryn know we'll be home earlier than expected, but then I decide I'd rather surprise them.

There's also another reason I'd rather not call. Along with trying to sort out everything concerning Danny's murder, I have to sort out my feelings for Gina.

After the divorce I told myself I'd never fall in love again. I wouldn't allow myself to fall in love again. Love takes too much energy. But since Gina and I started spending so much time together, I'm starting to rethink that.

I'm not saying I'm in love with Gina. It's too early for that. But I think I could possibly fall in love with her if I let myself. She's smart. She's funny. She's beautiful. She's kind, considerate, open-minded. I could go on and on.

Two of the most important things, though, are Kathryn adores her. She adores Kathryn.

I think she likes me a lot, too.

But, like I said, it's way too early to think about love. Before I can even think about that anymore, we both need to concentrate on finding out who killed Danny Dwyer. Until that mystery is solved neither one of us will have peace.

I need the peace to get on with my life. She needs the peace so she can write her article, leave *The Century* and get on with the rest of her life, follow her dream.

Just from the little bit she's told me about working there, I know it depresses her. She enjoys writing. She enjoys meeting new people. But she's frustrated with the way Alex is running the newsroom. She thinks he has his own agenda, which doesn't necessarily fit in with what's best for the paper.

I'm sure Gina will have a lot of thinking and soul searching to do before she leaves the paper. That is, if she decided leaving is the best thing for her. But if she does leave after writing the Danny Dwyer article, at least she'll go out with a bang.

With all the soul searching she'll probably be doing, the last thing she needs is a guy like me telling her he loves her.

**\*\*\*\*\*\*\*\*\*\*\***

On the drive back home Richie and I rehash everything we talked about the night before during dinner. We also take turns driving and sleeping.

At one point during the drive, my cell phone wakes me up. It's Gina telling me she just had a strange conversation with former police chief Bob Needham.

"No," she says, "He called me. It really caught me by surprise, and not just because of the call. It was the fact that he called on your home phone, not my cell phone."

"How would he know that you're at my house?" I ask.

"He didn't really say," Gina tells me. "When I asked him, he kind of stuttered and stammered for a quite a few seconds, but never really gave me a straight answer."

"That's odd," I say. "So, what did he want?"

"First, he asked if I was still digging into the Dwyer murder. When I told him I was, he was quiet for a few seconds. Then he told me to be careful that I might not want to dig to too far. When I told him I wasn't going to stop digging until I found some answers, he told me again to be careful."

"He didn't elaborate at all?" I ask.

"Not really. He was very cryptic. He kept saying things like …

Answers can be dangerous."

"Very interesting," I say.

"Yeah. Kind of scary, too."

"Are you too scared to keep going? If you are, I totally understand …"

"No way!," she says. "I'm in this 'til the end. We've come too far to give up now."

"That's my girl," I say, then immediately regret having said it. Until I hear her giggle. I swear I can almost feel her blushing.

"We're in this together," she says, with a lilt in her voice. She sounds like a giddy teen-ager and I can't help but smile. "I'm not going to let you finish this without me."

"Good," I say. "I'll see you when we get home."

I want to tell her I'll be home in a few hours, but I still think the surprise will be better so I keep it a secret.

I tell Richie what Gina just told me, then close my eyes to let in all sink in and try to make some sense of it. Before I know it, I'm asleep again and dreaming about Gina. A nice change from the nightmares about Danny.

We no sooner get back into town than Richie wakes me up and tells me he has a hunch of his own and to bear with him. He drives up to my house, but instead of stopping the car, he tells me to look at my watch and start timing. He drives to Kathryn's school. Seventeen minutes.

Richie drives back to my house. Again, he doesn't turn the engine off. He starts driving again and tells me to start timing again. We drive over a set of railroad tracks, past the oil refinery, over another set of railroad tracks. We drive a couple more minutes before pulling into the parking lot of Brafferd Buick, formerly known as David Dwyer Buick and Cadillac. I look at my watch. Eighteen minutes.

"Some hunch," I say.

"Your daughter could grow up to be a pretty good detective," Richie says. "How many kids her age would have known to equate the time she was in that car to the time it takes to get to school? And under those circumstances yet. She's something else."

"She sure is," I say.

"Do we dare have a look around?" Richie asks.

Although I want to check the place out, I'm a little nervous about it. It's getting dark. The place is closed. Of course that's the best time for snooping and investigating, but it could be risky.

"What if someone sees us lurking around and calls the police?" I ask.

"I am the police," Richie says.

Neither of us knows exactly what we're looking for, we both just feel the need to look. We stop at the door to a warehouse but decide against trying to open it in case we activate an alarm. We stop at another door to what looks like a garage. Again, we decide not to try the door.

But I know Richie's thinking what I'm thinking. Without even seeing the inside of either of these buildings, we know they could easily match the limited description Kathryn gave us of where she was held during the kidnapping.

"I have another hunch," Richie says, walking toward a back lot filled with old cars that look as if they're in dire need of repair before being either put on the lot or trashed.

"What is it this time?" I ask.

"You'll see," he says. "If I'm right, you'll see."

I follow Richie as he walks down the rows of cars, occasionally shining a flashlight on a car here and a car there. After a three rows, I notice a pattern. He's shining the flashlight on all the dark blue and black cars.

"Are you thinking what I think you're thinking?" I ask, after noticing the pattern.

"I think so," he says. "I don't know why I'm thinking it, but when we got here, it hit me."

"You're probably thinking it for the same reason I am," I say. "This place fits the description Kathryn gave us. If it's connected to the kidnapping, there's a chance it could be connected to Gina's so-called accident."

"A damn good chance," Richie says, shining his flashlight on the crushed side bumper of a dark blue LeSabre.

We both move in closer to get a better look at the damage. Sure enough. Green paint chips the same color as Gina's Mustang.

"Hidden in plain sight," Richie says, shaking his head. "Smart move."

"But not smart enough," I say.

"I don't suppose you know if Vaughn and Valentine own this place, do you?" Richie asks.

"As far as I know, the owner is a Jack Kirkland," I say. "But you know as well as I do that doesn't mean anything. First thing in the morning we'll have to see what we can find out about this Jack Kirkland."

"I'd bet almost anything there's a connection to Vaughn or Valentine," Richie says.

"Me too," I say. "The last thing we needed was another piece to this puzzle though."

"Let's look on the bright side," Richie says. "This may be the piece of the puzzle that makes all the other pieces fit."

# Chapter Twenty-eight

I find it a bit peculiar that all the lights are off in my house. But then I remind myself that Kathryn and Gina are probably doing exactly what I told them to do and getting some rest. I'll let them a sleep a little longer before I let them know I'm home.

On my way to the bathroom I flip on a couple of lights then check phone messages. Nothing. I take a quick look at the mail. A couple of bills. I smile. All is well.

I brush my teeth, splash some cold water on my face then head to the kitchen for a cold drink. There, under a cluster-of-shells refrigerator magnet Kathryn and I bought during our last trip to Ocean City, I find a note in my daughter's handwriting.

"We went to dinner with Mom. I miss you. See you went we get home. Love, Kat."

I told them to stay put and not open the door for anyone. I mean anyone. Not even Vanessa. I don't know if I'm angry because Kathryn and Gina aren't here, or if I'm angry because they're with Vanessa.

I'm confused as to why Kathryn would want to spend time with Vanessa. Last time we talked about Vanessa, Kathryn made it quite clear she didn't want anything to do with her mother. But, she is eight years old and maybe she realized she does need her mother at a time like this. It's not as if I want the two of them to spend no time together at all. I'm just confused as to what caused Kathryn's sudden change of heart.

I'm also a little bit confused as to why Vanessa would invite Gina along. Knowing that Kathryn isn't alone with Vanessa makes me feel a little better, but it doesn't make sense that Vanessa would want Gina there. Then again, not much that Vanessa does makes sense.

I look at the clock. It's 9:08 p.m. I suppose that's not terribly late for Kathryn to be out. I decide to take a shower and put on some clean comfortable clothes. If they're not back by the time I'm finished, I'll give them a call.

It's now 9:35 p.m. I can't believe Vanessa would keep Kathryn out this late on a school night. I was planning on keeping Kathryn out of school again tomorrow anyway. But still. It's the principle of the thing.

Theoretically, she doesn't really have to bring Kathryn back to my house. She has custody and, despite what Kathryn says she wants, Vanessa has the legal right to keep her there. It would be just like Vanessa to do that, no matter what Kathryn says.

But that's no excuse for not bringing Gina back here.

I call Vanessa's house. She answers on the third ring.

"Are you planning on bringing Kathryn home anytime soon?" I ask.

"May I remind you that this, not there, is Kathryn's home."

"Whatever," I say, trying to contain my anger. "Can I talk to her?"

"She's not here," Vanessa says. "They should have been back by now."

"What are you talking about? You didn't bring them home?"

"No. After dinner, we came back here for dessert. When it was time for Kathryn and what's-her-name to go, Randy said there was no need for me to leave the house again. Since it was on his way, he'd drop them off on his way home."

"Who's Randy?" I ask.

"Randy Bishop. He's a friend."

"I suggest you call your friend and find out what he did with my daughter, then call me back immediately."

I slam down the phone, knocking a picture off the table as I do. I pace waiting for Vanessa's call.

About a minute later she calls back.

"There's no answer at Randy's house," Vanessa says.

"When did they leave?" I ask.

"About 45 minutes ago."

"Forty-five minutes? It only takes 20 minutes to get from your house to mine."

"I'm aware of that," Vanessa says.

"Where does this Randy Bishop live?" I ask.

"On Washington Street. I'm not exactly sure of the address."

"Of course you wouldn't be."

"What's that supposed to mean?"

"Forget it. You just keep trying to get a hold of him and let me know if you do."

"What are you going to do?"

"Never mind. You just stay put and keep trying to get a hold of Randy Bishop."

The first thing I do after slamming down the phone again is call Gina's cell phone. I get her voice mail. Not a good sign. I leave a message anyway, telling her to call me back immediately. Next, I call Richie Banks and tell him what's going on.

"Another kidnapping?" he asks.

"I don't know what else to think at this point," I say.

"I hear ya, man. So, what did Vanessa tell you about this Bishop guy?"

"Just his name and that he lives somewhere on Washington Street."

"That's something. I'll see what I can do with it. You stay where you are and I'll call you … better yet … I'll come over as soon as I find out anything."

"Thanks man."

"No problem."

Waiting is definitely not one of the things I do best. I make a pot of coffee and pace while it brews. I pace while I'm drinking the first cup, then the second. I decide a third cup wouldn't be wise at this point. I'm already a nervous wreck. The last thing I need is more caffeine.

I can't stop thinking about Kathryn. She's already been through this once. How is she going to handle it again if, in fact, we're talking about another kidnapping. If that is the case, I hope the sick bastards who are behind this at least let her and Gina stay together.

If I could concentrate, I'd try to put those puzzle pieces together somehow. I know there's something missing, something we're just not seeing, but I can't put my finger on it.

Maybe I'm thinking too hard, making this too complicated. Look at the car that Richie and I believe forced Gina over the bank and into that ditch. It was hidden in plain sight. What if all the answers are that simple? What if I'm digging so deep that I'm missing the answer that's right on the surface?

I sit down for the first time in more than hour. I can sit still, but I can't pace anymore either. I need to do something, anything to find Kathryn and Gina. But what? I know the best thing to do is wait here until Richie gets here, but I feel helpless doing that. There's got to be something I can do.

I call Vanessa. She answers on the second ring.

"Randy?" she asks, without even saying "hello" first.

"No. It's me. I take it you haven't heard from him yet."

"No. Have you heard anything?"

"No."

"This is all your fault, you know," she says.

"My fault? How the hell is this my fault?"

"You and that whole Danny Dwyer case. It's all your fault Kathryn's missing and …"

"Stop right there," I say. "There's a very good possibility Kathryn's disappearance is related to Danny Dwyer, but I'm not the one who let this happen. Not this time or the first time."

"You're saying this is my fault?"

"You were the last one to see Kathryn … both times."

I hear her sniffling. I'm not sure if she's really crying or faking it. It's always hard to tell with Vanessa.

"Don't cry," I say, just in case it's the real thing. "Crying, shouting and blaming each other isn't going to help us find Kathryn."

"You're right," she says. "So, what can we do?"

"You can tell me everything you know about Randy Bishop."

"I really don't know him that well," she says.

That doesn't surprise me. Vanessa isn't exactly the choosy type when it comes to men, and conversation isn't her main priority in her so-called relationships. I wish I would have listened to the people who told me that before we got married.

Be that as it may, she tells me what she does know about Randy Bishop. Somehow, I'm not surprised to learn that he's a mechanic at Brafferd County Buick. I really don't want to know anymore about him. I tell Vanessa to let me know if Randy contacts her. I promise to keep her informed of any developments, although I don't intend on telling her anything until Kathryn's safe and sound. What Vanessa doesn't know won't her. What she does know could hurt Kathryn.

I no sooner get off the phone with Vanessa than there's a knock at my front door. It's Richie. He gathered the same information I did about Randy Bishop, but not much more. The only added information he has is that Bishop moved here from West Virginia. I'm not surprised to hear that either.

Richie tells me that it would be nearly impossible to find out anymore about Randy Bishop without contacting someone at Brafferd County Buick. If we do that, and they are, as we suspect, involved in the Danny Dwyer murder cover-up, we'd be tipping them off. We'd also be in way over our heads and possibly endangering Kathryn and Gina even further.

Richie suggests that it's time we bring the police in on this officially. Reluctantly, I agree.

# Chapter Twenty-nine

One of the downsides to bringing the police in on this is that they want me out of the picture. I tell Richie I can't spend anymore time drinking coffee, pacing and waiting. I need to be involved.

He discusses this with his superior officers and, amazingly enough, they agree that I can ride along with Richie - if I keep my mouth shut and don't make waves. That will be difficult, but I agree.

It was especially difficult when they talked about getting search warrants for Randy Bishop's house and the entire grounds of Brafferd County Buick. Proper procedure is getting the warrants by way of the judge. In this case, however, it's obvious they can't go to Judge Vaughn. At least it was obvious to Richie and me.

It took us nearly half an hour - half an hour we could have been looking for Kathryn and Gina - to convince them to go to a judge from another county. We didn't even feel comfortable with them asking Judge Cleland. The only way we would feel comfortable is if they went to a judge from another county. Yes, there's more red tape involved, but under the circumstances there's no other choice. We can't let Judge Vaughn know the police are involved. He's in on this cover-up somehow - Richie and I are sure of it. We just need to prove it. We can't let him tip off the other people involved.

While we're wasting time arguing about search warrants, at least some of the police officers are doing something constructive. They're doing another check on Randy Bishop and checks on Jack Kirkland, the owner of Brafferd County Buick.

As soon as the search warrants are issued, two officers are sent to Randy Bishop's house. Richie calls Jack Kirkland and tells him to meet us at the dealership. On the drive from the station to the dealership, Richie and I fill his partner in on everything we learned.

His partner, Rob French, was briefed on everything, just as all the other officers were, but he still finds it hard to believe. I imagine a lot of people do, and will once word of this gets around. It's not every day that a judge and a district attorney scheme to hinder a murder investigation, especially in small town America.

We get to Brafferd County Buick about ten minutes before Jack Kirkland arrives. We wait in the patrol car, not saying a word, until Kirkland pulls up next to us and gets out of his car.

"What's this all about, Officer?" Kirkland asks Richie.

"Two people were kidnapped this evening," Richie says, "and we have reason to believe they're being held here."

"Here?" Kirkland asks. "Why would kidnappers bring someone here?"

"That's one of things we're trying to find out," Richie says.

The four of us walk over to the warehouse, one of the two places we believe Kathryn was held, before. Kirkland unlocks the door, steps inside and turns on the lights. We look around and find nothing but boxes of automotive supplies and parts. I don't know if anyone else noticed this, but I did. There's not a restroom in the building. Kathryn said there was a restroom in the place they had her.

After Richie says we're finished in the warehouse, Kirkland turns off the lights and locks up. We head for the garage and auto body shop.

Again, Kirkland unlocks the door, steps inside and turns on the lights.

The building appears empty except for the normal items one would find in a mechanic's garage and auto body shop. Still, we look around.

Richie opens a door that reveals a small, dirty restroom. He looks at me. He must have been thinking the same thing I was in the warehouse. That couldn't have been where Kathryn was held, but this could be. We dig through an overflowing trashcan in the corner. There's a half-eaten piece of pepperoni pizza near the bottom.

Richie sends Rob out to the car to get a camera. When he returns, Richie takes dozens of pictures of the garage, the restroom, the trash can.

Kirkland keeps asking questions. No one answers him.

Richie gets a call on his radio from one of the officers sent to Randy Bishop's house. Bishop was home. Alone. He claims he dropped Kathryn and Gina off at my house then went out for a drink before going back home. He claims that when he got home he unplugged his phone because he wanted to sleep without any interruptions. That's why he didn't answer when Vanessa called.

No one is buying his story.

Richie, Rob and the other cops who arrived on the scene, along with those on the radio, decide they need to regroup. Despite my objections, I'm not invited to sit in on the conference. Richie promises he'll fill me in on everything when they're finished. I trust that he will, but that doesn't make the waiting any easier.

While the cops are mapping out their game plan, Kathryn and Gina are being held against their will somewhere. At least that's the assumption. What else can we assume at this point?

I hope and pray that Kathryn and Gina aren't being treated badly. Although the first kidnapping was traumatic for Kathryn, and will most likely leave emotional scars, it seems she wasn't treated badly. I suppose I should say she wasn't treated badly under the circumstances.

But I do know that these people - whoever these people are - are capable of violence. Look what they did to Gina. She could have been killed, or at least seriously injured. She was lucky to escape with only a few bumps, bruises and a broken wrist.

Who's to say she and Kathryn will be that lucky this time?

To make time go by faster while the cops are doing their thing, and to stop from thinking the worst about what's happening to Kathryn and Gina, I decide to chat with Jack Kirkland while I'm waiting. If I keep it casual, no one can say I'm interfering with the investigation.

"What's this all about?" Kirkland asks me.

"I really can't say."

"Obviously, the police think someone here is involved in a kidnapping. Can you at least tell me who it is?" he asks.

"No," I say. "I really can't. I shouldn't even be here. I know I shouldn't be talking to you. I don't want to give the police any reason to make me leave."

"Don't they have to tell me what this is all about?" Kirkland asks.

"I'm sure they will eventually."

"I'm sure if they don't, my uncle will have something to say about all this," Kirkland says.

"Who's your uncle?" I ask.

"Warren Vaughn."

"Judge Warren Vaughn?" I ask, not sure I heard him correctly.

"Yes," Kirkland says. "Judge Warren Vaughn."

I'm dumbfounded. The missing piece to the puzzle was, in fact, right here in plain sight.

It seems we have all the pieces now. The hard part will be fitting them all together.

# Chapter Thirty

I have to say that sometimes following proper police procedures sucks. Kathryn and Gina are somewhere out there, but the police are at a standstill because they're following the rules and taking it slow.

If I wasn't so worried that Kathryn and Gina might be harmed, I suppose I'd be glad the police are making sure they don't make mistakes. This thing has been covered up for almost 30 years. If they don't do everything right this time, it's possible the truth will never come out.

I've had just about all the coffee I can handle. What I really need right now is a shot or two or five of whiskey - especially after talking to Vanessa. I didn't want to call, but I felt I at least owed her that much. Hard as it is for me to fathom, I suppose she could possibly have an iota of maternal instinct hidden somewhere. Although both times Kathryn was kidnapped she was - and I use this phrase loosely - in Vanessa's care, I can't hold that against her. Not now anyway. First, I had to let her know where the investigation stands. I'll hit her with the guilt later.

It's possible that the kidnappings could work against her during the custody hearing. But then again, her lawyer could argue that the kidnappings wouldn't have occurred if not for my involvement in this case.

I could drive myself crazy thinking about the custody hearing. Instead, I'll drive myself crazy wondering where Kathryn and Gina are and how they're being treated. I hope they're together. I hope they're able to talk to each other and keep each other strong. I hate to think of either one of them going through this alone.

I wish the police could speed this up somehow. No one's been here to update me in more than an hour. The assistant chief's office, where they decided I'd be out of the way, has no windows so I'm pretty much staring at the four pale yellow concrete block walls, bare except for a clock. Thinking. Worrying. Checking the time. Getting angrier by the minute.

The sun should be coming up in a couple of hours. Kathryn and Gina will have spent all night who-knows-where with who-knows-who doing who-knows-what to them. That's totally unacceptable to me, but there's nothing I can do about it.

I suppose I could try to find them on my own, but that could be dangerous, not just for me but for Kathryn and Gina.

So, I wait.

Another half an hour passes before Richie comes in to give me another update. It's not exactly what I wanted to hear.

They searched Randy Bishop's house and car. They found nothing in his house. They did, however, find hair samples that could be Kathryn's and Gina's but that doesn't really mean anything. Randy drove them and Vanessa to dinner, so naturally there would be signs Kathryn and Gina had been in his car.

Bishop still insists he dropped Kathryn and Gina off at my house then went to a bar for a couple of drinks. Although the bartender does remember Bishop being there, he doesn't remember what time he got there. Richie tells me that later in the day they'll try tracking down some of the other people who were there to see if they remember what time Bishop arrived.

Richie also tells me the police talked to my neighbors. None of them remember seeing Kathryn and Gina being dropped off, but they all admit they weren't paying attention. One of the things I like about the neighborhood is that the neighbors aren't nosy. I never thought that would be a disadvantage.

On to Jack Kirkland. Richie says no one can tell if he's being difficult or if he really doesn't know anything. He claims he doesn't know anything about the car in the lot that, we assume, was used to force Gina off the road. He further claims that the first time he saw the car was when the police showed it to him a few hours ago. He gives several scenarios of how the car could have gotten to his lot.

They all seem plausible, Richie says.

Now, they're just trying to keep him there until they can come up with a reason to bring Judge Vaughn and Bill Valentine in for questioning. They don't want to release Kirkland and give him the opportunity to tip Vaughn off before they're ready.

The problem is, Richie tells me, they can't find a reason to bring Vaughn and Valentine in. The checks sent from David Dwyer Buick and Cadillac to WV Quality Cars isn't enough. They really aren't anything at all unless we can connect the money to the murder.

Richie tells me Kirkland said there are plenty of reasons one car dealership could be sending checks to another. They all make perfect sense. Damn.

I don't care how legitimate the passing of money could be, I know there was something shady going on. I can feel it. I just have to figure out what that something is.

# Chapter Thirty-one

After much prodding and persuasion from Richie, the police chief decides the money - the suspect checks - is enough reason to question Judge Vaughn and Bill Valentine after all. He says they'll do their best to question them without accusing them of any wrongdoing. If possible, they won't even mention the kidnapping or the murder. They'll simply say they're working on a case.

I'm not overly comfortable with that. Vaughn and Valentine are smarter than that. If they are involved in the kidnapping and murder, they'll see right through the story that the police are simply working on any old case. Natural paranoia would tell them that.

Because they don't want to raise suspicion, the police ask me to either stay at the station or go home. I agree that's a good idea. If Vaughn and Valentine saw me and they are involved in all of this, they would know what the police are after. I decide home is the best place for me right now.

Once I get there, I call Vanessa again. I guess I'm too tired to get angry with her. When she tells me, yet again, that this is all my fault I just tell her I'll call if I hear anything else and I hang up the phone. I don't need to hear that at this point, least of all from her.

After getting rid of her for the time being, I take a shower. I figure it might calm me down and reverse some of the effects of the caffeine I've been pouring down my throat for the last several hours.

I no sooner get out of the shower and put on fresh clothes when the phone rings. The person on the other end is obviously trying to disguise his voice when he says "We warned you."

"Don't hang up," I beg, shouting into the phone. "What do you want? I'll do anything to get them back safely."

"Call off the police," the voice says before ending the call.

I immediately call Richie.

"It's too late to back off now," Richie says. "The best we can do now is find them before ..."

"Before the bastards kill them," I say, feeling myself getting out of control.

"We'll do everything we can to make sure that doesn't happen. ... I don't know if this is the best time to tell you this ..."

"Tell me what?"

"We're at Judge Vaughn's house. His wife just told us he's out of town on a business trip."

"Business trip my ass. He's running."

"That would be my guess. After she told us that, we called the DA's office to get Valentine's schedule. He called in sick today. We sent a car to his house. He's not there."

"Damn! How did they find out?"

"My guess would be Kevin Harper. Or it could have been Bob Needham. When Gina tried talking to him again, he knew the two of you hadn't given up. One of them must have told them you were snooping again. That must be why Gina and Kathryn ... why that happened."

"I knew there was a reason I didn't trust those guys. Never did trust them."

"There is a positive side to this," Richie says.

"Oh yeah? What would that be?"

"Vaughn and Valentine are running. Why would they be running if they're not involved? Seems like a mighty big coincidence that both of them are missing just as we're closing in on this."

"I guess you're right," I say. "But that doesn't help find Kathryn and Gina."

"No, it doesn't. But we're working on that. We're waiting for search warrants to get into Vaughn's house and Valentine's. We've also alerted the Elkins, West Virginia, police. I haven't gotten an update yet as to what's happening on that front, but I thought you should know we're working on it."

Knowing what's going on eases a little bit of the tension, but I still feel helpless just sitting here. I get in my car and make the 45-minute drive to Judge Vaughn's house.

Richie tells me I shouldn't be there, but says he knows there would be no point in telling me to go back home. He tells me they just got the search warrant a few minutes ago so they haven't found anything yet. They've decided to check the grounds of the old farm the judge bought and converted to his liking about 20 years ago. After checking the grounds, they'll move inside the house. I follow Richie to what used to be a barn that's a few hundred feet behind the garage.

I gasp as soon as I set foot inside the building. Gina's perfume. Chantilly. The smell is as strong as it would be if she was standing right next to me. Obviously, she's not. There's nothing in the building. It's totally empty except for the scent of Chantilly. Despite everything, I smile. I have a gut feeling Gina must have sprayed the perfume as a way of leaving a trail. Good thinking.

Now that we know Gina was here, we have to find out where they went from here. I'm assuming it's "they," that Gina and Kathryn are still together. That's one of the thoughts that's keeping me going.

Despite objections by some of the police officers, I'm allowed to follow Richie around during the search of the house.

Our assignment is to start in the judge's study. We couldn't have gotten a better place to search if we'd asked for it.

I start at the judge's desk while Richie goes through the file cabinets. I wish I could get into his computer. I bet there's something incriminating there. But since I can't access his computer files, I'll try not to concentrate on it - for the moment anyway.

I'm not interested in seeing anything current in the judge's desk. I'm looking for anything dating back to the time of Danny's murder. I'm hoping the judge is as much of a packrat as he seems to be. The entire study is lined with books, folders and various other forms of memorabilia and paraphernalia. I'm hoping all of this preservation of the judge's history goes back far enough to help with this case.

It would help if all of this was arranged in some kind of order. Alphabetical. Chronological. It wouldn't matter. Anything would be nice, but beggars can't be choosers. Of course the cliché makes me think of Gina even more. But I know I can't think of her that way right now. I have to think only of digging up some kind of information, some clue that will help me find her and my daughter.

After about an hour of searching, I finally come across something that might be helpful. It's an old notebook - pages yellowed and dog-eared - with the name "Dwyer" scribbled on the cover.

My hands shake as I flip through the pages. I know I should start at the beginning, but I'm hoping that during my skimming something will pop out at me. Nothing does. Maybe it's because I'm too nervous, too anxious, too worried that I won't find something useful in time to help Kathryn and Gina.

I decide that no matter how fast I want this to go, the best course of action is taking it slow and starting from the beginning. I turn on the desk lamp, pull my chair closer and settle in for the long haul.

Just as I'm about to start reading, a state police trooper enters the room. It seems my prayers were answered. He tells Richie and me that he's here to try to gain access to the judge's computer. Hallelujah! I know there will be something useful there. I just know it. Neither Richie nor I saw any computer disks in the room so, unless the judge took disks with him - or destroyed them - everything we need to know should, in theory, be accessible once the trooper gets in.

I'm trying to ignore what the trooper is doing and concentrate on the notebook. After reading two handwritten pages I come to the conclusion it's a diary of sorts. Exactly what I was hoping to find.

It doesn't take long - about five pages - for me to come to another conclusion. Judge Warren Vaughn hated David Dwyer. Okay. Maybe hated is too strong a word. Resented is probably more accurate.

It seems that when Judge Vaughn first came to Brafferd County, he and Bill Valentine planned on branching out and opening another WV Quality Cars dealership. But through their contacts at the country club and civic organizations they learned that competing against David Dwyer in any business venture wasn't a wise idea.

Dwyer was one of the wealthiest and most powerful men in the county, not to mention popular. At that time, you would have been hard pressed to find anyone who would say a bad word about him.

According to the judge's makeshift diary, it didn't take him and Valentine long to learn that going against David Dwyer in any way, shape or form could hurt them - not only in business, but in the futures they planned in politics. But they vowed to each other that they'd find a way to either run Dwyer out of the county or, at least, find a way to hurt his business enough that he wouldn't be a threat to them.

Apparently, according to the judge's diary, Dwyer learned of their plan and assured Vaughn and Valentine they would never hurt his business because of his status in the community.

This, naturally, made Vaughn and Valentine even more determined to ruin David Dwyer.

In the years that followed, Vaughn and Valentine were content "working our plan," as the judge wrote. The notes for these years were sparse and disjointed but, from what I gather, the plan was for them to make themselves as popular as David Dwyer.

They joined all the clubs and organizations Dwyer belonged to. They buttered up to all the other important - and rich - people in the county, especially those who would be helpful when election time rolled around.

But no matter how hard they tried, they couldn't seem to find a way to sway anyone's loyalty away from Dwyer. The more they tried and failed the angrier they got. They became more and more determined to bring WV Quality Cars to Brafferd County and run Dwyer's business into the ground.

They knew, though, that the climate wasn't right yet. They knew that if they brought their dealership into the county and competed against Dwyer their political careers were over. It was even possible that their legal careers in the county would be over as well.

The only thing they could do, according to the judge's diary, was stay on the same path and wait for the climate to change.

Several more years passed before the climate did change. It was then that Kevin Harper enrolled in University of Pittsburgh Brafferd. Only a few weeks after being on campus, he was picked up for dealing drugs on campus. His grandfather, Bill Valentine, pulled some strings. Kevin was never charged and went about his business.

He was picked up several more times, but never charged. Valentine eventually decided it was time to have a serious talk with his grandson and explain what could happen to both of them if people started gossiping about all of this. During the talk, Valentine learned that one of Kevin Harper's biggest customers was Danny Dwyer.

After a little bit of digging, Valentine learned that David Dwyer was pulling a few strings of his own to make sure his son wasn't arrested. "It just wouldn't do for the son of the county's golden boy (Dwyer) to be a common drug addict," the judge wrote in his diary.

The climate just changed.

According to the judge's diary, he and Valentine weren't as concerned as they had been about bringing WV Quality Cars to Brafferd County. That venture was now taking a back seat to putting David Dwyer through hell.

The new plan was to have Dwyer finance Vaughn and Valentine's new car dealership in Brafferd County. If he paid them $20,000 a month, they'd keep quiet about Danny's drug use. When they had enough money to buy the property they wanted, construct the necessary buildings, stock the lot and buy everything else they needed to start the business, Dwyer would announce his retirement, thus paving the way for Vaughn and Valentine to open their business with no repercussions from the community that adored David Dwyer.

Two years into the plan, the climate started changing again.

As near as I can figure, the snag in the plan came during the two weeks - about two weeks before he died - that Danny was clean and sober. I remember that time very well. I don't know how long Danny had been clean before he knocked on the front door of my parent's house that day, but he looked like a different person. No. He looked like the Danny I'd known my whole life. He told me he needed to get away. We spent the next week at his father's house on the lake. I don't remember everything we talked about, but I do remember that Danny said he needed to make a new start - for himself and for his father.

He never explained to me what his father had to do with it. At the time, I assumed he wanted to change out of love and respect for his father. Maybe that was part of it. Now I know the rest.

The fact that Danny was clean and sober not long before he died made his foray back into the drug scene even more confusing. Now, thanks to the judge's diary, I'm beginning to understand what happened.

I can't believe two grown men would use people this way just to make money. Bastards.

Although not in so many words, the judge's diary says that Kevin Harper wouldn't give up on Danny. He kept stopping by Danny's house trying to get him hooked again. Vaughn and Valentine knew that without Danny's drug use to hang over Dwyer's head, their money tree was gone. Apparently, Valentine even threatened his own grandson with jail if he didn't get Danny hooked again.

The last entry in the diary is dated the day after Danny's murder. It reads "The shit hit the fan. Needham better not crack."

Another question answered. Apparently it was Vaughn and/or Valentine who told Needham to rule Danny's death a suicide. They must have gotten to the coroner as well.

But the big questions are still unanswered. Who killed Danny Dwyer? Where are Kathryn and Gina?

# Chapter Thirty-two

"It doesn't make sense," Richie says, after I tell him what I just read in the judge's diary. "Vaughn and Valentine are rich men. Why would they blackmail David Dwyer and use Danny and Kevin that way just to bring a new business to Brafferd County?"

"Who knows?" I say. "Greed does strange things to people. It's hard to explain."

"Or maybe they're just sick bastards," Richie says.

"I think they're sick bastards no matter how you look at it," I say.

"I just don't get it," Richie says. "There are thousands of places between here and West Virginia where they could have opened a new business. Why here? Why did they go through all that trouble to open the business here?"

"Simple," I say. "I'm paraphrasing here, but the judge wrote that no one had ever said 'no' to him and Valentine. No one had ever told them they couldn't do something …"

"And when someone did say no," Richie says, "they cracked. They didn't know how to deal with it and just went overboard."

"Seems that way," I say. "Add that to the fact that they both had some power and you have a lethal mix. Literally. … And before two more people are …"

"We have to find Gina and Kathryn," Richie says. "We will. We called the West Virginia State Police. As we speak, they're searching every WV Quality Cars. They've also issued APBs concerning Vaughn, Valentine and Kevin Harper, as well as another Amber Alert on Kathryn. We're working on it. Believe me. We're working on it."

"I believe you," I say. "I'm just praying that it's not too late."

"Keep praying," Richie says.

"That doesn't sound very encouraging," I say. "I guess that means you haven't found anything."

"Not a thing," Richie says, going back to the file cabinet. He slams a drawer shut then opens another and starts flipping through the files. "Well, well, well. What do we have here?"

"What?" I ask.

"A file marked 'real estate records,'" Richie says, a hopeful smile covering his face.

I stand behind Richie and look over his shoulder while he goes through the file.

"Man," Richie says. "This guy owns half of West Virginia. If Gina and Kathryn are on any of his properties, it could take us weeks to find them."

"We don't have weeks," I say. "We better start moving now … and pray Valentine doesn't own as much property as Vaughn."

Our prayers weren't answered that time. After calling the cops searching Valentine's house and telling them to look for real estate records, we learn that what Vaughn doesn't own, Valentine does. In all, there are more than 500 properties - commercial and residential - Vaughn and Valentine own either jointly or by themselves.

The search for Kathryn and Gina will be more time-consuming than anyone anticipated. Now all we can do is hope and pray they're being held on one of those properties. Keeping them on one of the properties Vaughn and Valentine own would be so obvious, but I've learned that sometimes it's the obvious that's most overlooked.

Let's hope Vaughn and Valentine are counting on that.

# Chapter Thirty-three

Now I'm standing behind the state trooper who is diligently trying to find something useful on the judge's computer. He broke the password and has been looking through file after file, but so far he's come up empty. He says after looking at the last file - which he's looking at right now - he'll try getting into the judge's e-mail.

He's already looked through Outlook Express, which wasn't password protected, but found little of value there. What he did find, however, was that the judge has an e-mail account at Hotmail. At least he assumes hizzonerwv@hotmail.com is the judge. At any rate, there was mail forwarded to that address from the Outlook Express address - judgevaughn@earthlink.net -- and it's worth checking out.

I think I've mentioned this before. I hate waiting. I'm not good at it. I need results, answers. Now. The only thing keeping me from getting totally obnoxious and driving everyone crazy at this point is thinking of Kathryn and Gina. I keep thinking that if the waiting is this hard for me, it must be unbearable for them. Again, I pray that, wherever they are, they're together.

Although I'm trying my best to stay calm, I think I'm driving the trooper at the computer crazy by tapping my fingers on the back of his chair. He's already turned around several times and glared at me. I decide if I don't want to get kicked out of the room, I better find some other release for my nervous energy. I go to the old standby. Pacing.

About fifteen minutes later, the trooper calls me over to the computer.

"I think I'm in," he says, watching the page on the computer screen load.

"Really?" I ask. I'm too brain dead to think of anything else to say.

"There it is," he says as the page loads and tells us hizzonerwv has 22 new messages in his inbox.

The trooper goes into the inbox. We see three e-mails dated yesterday from wv_the_da. That's got to be Bill Valentine, we think. We open the first one, hoping that previous messages are included in this one. They are. We read from the bottom up, starting with a message written by the judge.

"I'm not going down because of this."

"No one's going down," Valentine wrote back. "It's under control."

"How?"

"Manzarelli will stop this time and call off the cops. Daughter and girlfriend."

"Details?"

"Bishop hands off to Butch and Smitty. They hand off to Kevin. He hands off to Bud and Henry."

"Where?"

"Don't know. Don't want to know. Know too much already."

"Keep me posted."

"Will do."

The trooper, Richie and I simply look at each other. Valentine obviously had a hand in planning the kidnapping - the kidnapping the judge knows about.

We move on to the next e-mail.

"JM didn't call off the cops. They're on the trail," Valentine wrote.

"Now what?" Vaughn wrote back.

"Regrouping."

The trooper, Richie and I look at each other again and shrug.

"What the hell does regrouping mean?" I ask.

"I don't know," Richie says. "I hate to say this and alarm you, but there's only one place to go after kidnapping. They, or their cohorts have already killed once so it's probably not beyond them to do it again."

"Then we have to find them," I say. "Now!"

"We will man," Richie says, placing a hand on my shoulder. "We will."

First, we read the last e-mail.

"I'll come to your house," the judge wrote. "Twenty minutes."

"I'll be ready in five."

That was it. No more messages. No previous messages. We don't know how or when the judge and Valentine found out we're on to them. All we know is that the e-mail was written at 2:56 a.m. Apparently they talked on the phone or in person first before planning their escape. If only there'd been time to wire their phones. Damn.

But we don't have time to think about the would haves and should haves. We have to find Kathryn and Gina before it's too late.

I also don't have time, or the inclination, to talk to Vanessa. But after my cell phone rings and I see that the call is from her, I decide it's probably best to give her an update.

"I'll never forgive you if something happens to Kathryn," Vanessa says after I tell her what's happening.

"I don't give a damn about your forgiveness," I say. "All I care about is finding her alive and well. Right now, you're keeping me from doing that."

"You'll pay for this Joe," she says. "Believe me, you'll pay for this."

"Vanessa, I'm not in the mood for your threats. I'm also not in the mood for any of your little power plays and games. We'll discuss this after Kathryn is home safely."

"You bet we will," she says before ending the call.

I don't know what I ever saw in that woman. Maybe one day I'll take the time to think about it - so I never make that mistake again. But right now I need to find Kathryn. And Gina.

# Chapter Thirty-four

The West Virginia State Police haven't come up with anything yet. So far, they've searched about two dozen of the 515 properties owned by Vaughn and Valentine, either separately or jointly.

Also, the search for Kevin Harper is a bust so far. A couple of cops have been sent to question Randy Bishop again. Since we know a little more about his involvement, we figure he'll be more willing to talk. Without the help of the district attorney, it's hard for the cops to be able to offer him a deal if he cooperates.

When the district attorney is a suspect in a murder investigation, the whole legal system is out of whack.

Without getting into detail, the police chief tells assistant district attorney Bethany Edwards he needs to be able to make some kind of deal with Bishop. Confused about why she's being called, and why Bill Valentine isn't available, she tells the chief to do what he thinks is best.

The chief tells his officers to simply tell Bishop the assistant DA will go easy on him if he cooperates. Seems safe enough although, because kidnapping is a federal charge the DA's office won't have all that much input.

During the questioning, which I watched and listened to behind a one-way window, Bishop at first insisted - still - that he didn't know anything. He says all he did was drop Kathryn and Gina off at my house after dinner and a visit at Vanessa's house.

But after about 45 minutes he became more helpful, whether he realized it or not.

He'd been seeing Vanessa for about two weeks. He said he wouldn't exactly call it dating because they'd only actually gone out twice - the day they met and the night they went out with Kathryn and Gina. The other times they saw each other it was at Vanessa's house.

Bishop said a guy he works with - Butch Yeager - suggested he asked Vanessa out in the first place. From what he could figure, Bishop said, Butch Yeager doesn't really know Vanessa, but from what he knew about her he thought she and Bishop would get along.

Bishop said he didn't understand why Yeager thought that. He admitted he didn't really like Vanessa all that much, but the sex was good.

Been there, done that, I thought to myself when he said that.

Bishop said he wasn't too thrilled about going to dinner with Vanessa and Kathryn but, again, it was Butch Yeager who pushed it. Yeager said oftentimes people act differently around their children. Yeager told Bishop that maybe he'd see Vanessa in a new light if he saw her with Kathryn.

The rest of the story stayed the same as it had been when Bishop was first questioned. After dinner and a stop at Vanessa's house, Bishop drove Kathryn and Gina to my house and dropped them off. That was the last he'd seen them.

From the sound of things, Bishop was simply a pawn in this whole mess. But at least he gave us someplace to go, someone else to question.

On to Butch Yeager.

He was quite easy to find. He was at work in the garage at Brafferd County Buick acting as if nothing had happened. My first impression was that he's not smart enough to be that good of an actor. Maybe he really doesn't know what's happening. Maybe he wasn't given the bigger picture.

Again, I watched the questioning on the other side of the window. At first he was very uncooperative. Hostile even. But it didn't take long for him to spill his guts after the police told him he was now involved in a murder investigation.

The police started out slow, trying to get the entire story from chapter one. Yeager said the reason he tried to hook up Randy Bishop with Vanessa is that his boss - Jack Kirkland, Judge Vaughn's nephew

- thought it would be a good idea. Yeager admitted that he thought Kirkland was pushing the Bishop/Vanessa hook up a little too hard, but he didn't ask questions. Kirkland is his boss and he did what he was told.

He didn't ask questions about the kidnapping either. He said he didn't think of it as a kidnapping until the police said the word out loud. He simply thought of it as following orders. Orders from whom, he wasn't sure.

Yeager said he got involved after getting a note in his locker with specific instructions on where to be at what time, and what to do. The note instructed him not to ask questions and said "it will be in your best interest, both personally and professionally, if you follow these instructions to the letter and not speak to anyone about it."

Smitty, a friend of Yeager's from work, was the other person who got exactly the same note. Some friend, I think. Yeager doesn't even know Smitty's first name.

"We didn't ask questions," Yeager told the police. "We were scared, ya know?"

He said he and Smitty waited outside my house until Bishop dropped Kathryn and Vanessa off. As soon as they were on the front porch, he and Smitty ran up and told them they were "going for a ride."

Kathryn told them she had to leave a note for me. Yeager and Smitty told her that wouldn't be necessary. He said Gina then asked if I knew where they were going, or had I sent them to take us somewhere. Yeager said he told Gina not to ask so many questions and that she would get all her answers soon enough.

"Me and Smitty didn't know exactly what we were doing," Yeager says, "but it sounded good. Tough, ya know?"

The police officers questioning him simply shake their heads. I want to break through the glass and pound the crap out of him. Thankfully, Richie and his partner Rob are on either side of me holding me back, keeping me calm. Keeping me sane. Correction. Somewhat calm and sane.

At least I know, for a while anyway, Kathryn and Gina were

together.

Yeager said after he and Smitty lead Kathryn and Gina to the car, Kathryn started crying. But after only a short time - not even a minute, Yeager says - she stopped and said she wasn't going to cry because " … that's what you guys want and I'm not going to give you what you want."

That's my girl, I say to myself.

Yeager goes on to say that, despite his warning, Gina kept asking questions.

That's my girl, too, I say, again, to myself.

"She was really getting on our nerves," Yeager says. "We didn't know anything and she keeps asking questions we didn't have the answers to. Even if we did have answers we probably wouldn't have told her. I'm only saying that because I have an idea of what's going on now. Then, I didn't have a clue. We just knew we were supposed to take them to the Eat 'n' Park restaurant in Bridgeport, West Virginia."

Another thing that told us we're on the right track - they went to West Virginia.

Rob leaves to go call the West Virginia State Police and tell them Kathryn and Gina were in Bridgeport. We all hope someone saw them there and can tell us where they went from there.

Yeager says the four of them went into the restaurant. He, Smitty and Gina ordered coffee. Kathryn had hot chocolate. Yeager and Smitty were about to order pie when a man introducing himself as Kevin Harper came up to their table. He pulled Yeager aside, told him to finish their drinks, let Kathryn and Gina use the restroom then meet him outside.

Yeager did what he was told.

Outside the restaurant, Yeager says, Harper walked up behind the four of them, grabbed onto Kathryn's and Gina's arms and lead them away to a dark corner of the parking lot. Yeager said he didn't see what kind of car Harper was driving or which way they went. He said he wasn't even sure he saw them drive away. He saw a car, he said. He just wasn't sure if it was them.

Talking to - interrogating? -- Yeager turned out to be fairly productive. If nothing else, at least we know we're on the right track. According the e-mail correspondence between the judge and Valentine, what we have to do to stay on the right track is find out who Bud and Henry are. They were supposed to get the "hand off" from Kevin Harper. If Kathryn and Gina are, in fact, the hand off as we assume they are, Bud and Henry are the end of the line and Kathryn and Gina are with them.

The officers doing the questioning are still with Yeager when we get word from the West Virginia State Police saying they found Kevin Harper. He's at home, but in the process of being put in a police car and taken to the state police barracks for questioning.

Richie and I are on our way to Elkins, West Virginia. Again.

# Chapter Thirty-five

Richie and I decide to save time it's better to fly than drive to West Virginia this time. The state police pick us up at the airport and drive us the 150 or so miles to the state police barracks where Kevin Harper is being held.

On the way, we learn that Harper isn't being the least bit cooperative. In the last five hours he hasn't said a word except to demand a lawyer. His lawyer - another relative, of course - has talked to police but hasn't allowed Kevin to talk.

The lawyer hasn't even made a phone call yet. Because all calls in and out of the barracks are monitored, the police were hoping he'd try to contact Valentine or Vaughn, thus leading them right to where they need to go. But so far he hasn't called anyone. He's barely even talked to Kevin.

When Richie and I arrive at the barracks, Kevin is in a holding room in view of the door we just passed through. I swear Kevin turned white as a ghost when he saw me. I'm pretty sure that wasn't my imagination.

"Is that Harper?" Richie whispers to me.

"Sure is," I say.

"Did you see the look on his face when we walked in?"

"Sure did," I say. "Guess I wasn't imagining it after all."

"The boy is scared," Richie says.

"Good."

I talk the state police into allowing me to help question Kevin Harper. Although it's a highly unusual procedure, they agree because they say I'm closer to the case than anyone. I'm also the only one with a personal stake in the outcome, but I knew better than to use that argument. I would probably be watching on the sidelines again if

169

I had. The last thing they need is an emotional father questioning this guy.

I'm surprised that the police let me take the lead in the questioning.

"First of all," I say to Kevin, "I want you to know I'm not here to ask questions about Danny Dwyer. My daughter is missing and I think your grandfather has something to do with it."

"In that case," Kevin says, "why don't you question my grandfather?"

"We can't find your grandfather," I tell him.

"I'd say that's your problem, not mine," he says.

"Well, you see Kevin, that's where you're wrong," I say. "I happen to know someone who says the last time he saw my daughter she was with you."

Kevin's lawyer, whose name I don't even want to know, butts in and tells him he doesn't have to say anything more.

"Fine," I say to the lawyer. "Let me lay out the story for you, then you can decide if your client should keep quiet and pay the consequences, or talk and hope for some kind of leniency."

"Fine," the lawyer says.

"Let me tell you a little story about greed, power and corruption," I say. "It's a story that leads to murder, attempted murder and kidnapping. We'd like the story to end before another murder or two is added to the story."

"Go on," the lawyer says.

"The story starts with two men who had the world at their feet from the day they were born," I say. They always got everything they wanted. No one ever said 'no' to them. Because of this gift or talent or whatever you want to call it, they became rich, powerful men. The more money they had, the more money they wanted. The more power they had, the more power they wanted. Money and power were their drugs.

"But one day someone did say 'no' to them and they didn't like it. Instead of taking it like men, they decided they weren't going to take it at all. They were going to teach this person a lesson."

"Stop right there," the lawyer says. "Just tell me what happened.

Don't give me any more of that this person and that person crap."

"Fine," I say. "Kevin Harper's grandfather, Bill Valentine is one of the greedy bastards. Judge Warren Vaughn is the other. You may know them as owners of WV Quality Cars, among other things. About 30 years ago they, along with your client, were involved in the murder of a college student who happened to be a friend of mine. Very few people knew about their involvement. No one was ever charge with my friend's murder. It remains unsolved to this day.

"However, a feisty newspaper reporter was asked to do a story on this unsolved murder. During the course of her research, she and I became friends. The deeper she started digging, the more she started leaning on me for help to figure out this mystery. She didn't want to write a story saying the murder was unsolved. Now she wanted to write a story saying the killer is behind bars.

"Now, that reporter and my daughter are missing. I won't tell you how we know this, but we know that Vaughn and Valentine are behind it."

Kevin's lawyer gives him a long look, then asks if he can talk to his client in private. I agree.

It seems we might be really getting somewhere this time. I continue to hope and pray it's not too late for Kathryn and Gina.

171

# Chapter Thirty-six

Kevin's lawyer comes out of the interrogation room and asks what kind of deal Kevin would get if he talks. I explain that because kidnapping is a federal offense neither I nor the Brentwood County District Attorney's office have the authority to offer deals. But I call the DA's office anyway, basically to placate Kevin and his lawyer. Anything to help me find Kathryn and Gina

The best Bethany Edwards can tell me is that prison time is a near certainty in a kidnapping case. But, she said, the feds may offer Kevin a lesser sentence at a minimum security facility.

Kevin's lawyer goes back in the interrogation room and tells him the news. He comes back out saying Kevin has agreed to tell us everything he knows.

"Joe, we've known each other for a lot of years," Kevin starts. "I'll admit, and I know you will, too, that we don't like each other or, at least we didn't back then. But all that aside, I have to tell you that if I knew where your daughter was right now, I would tell you. I have a couple of kids of my own, and I can't even imagine what you're going through."

"Be that as it may," I say, "you're one of the people who's putting me through this. So, if you'll stop with all the apologies and empty words to ease your conscious, I'd appreciate it if you'd tell us something that will help us find Kathryn."

He glares at me with the angry look I knew all too well during the days of Danny's drug use, but starts talking anyway.

"You pretty much hit the nail on the head with the murder story," he says. "The part you left out was ... When Danny was clean and sober for that short time right before he was killed, he found out exactly what was happening and threatened to go public with everything. Until the day he died he said my grandfather and Judge Vaughn wouldn't get away with blackmailing his father.

"But that's ancient history now. Getting back to your daughter, my grandfather was scared when he called me with the plans, although he would never admit he was scared. But, after hearing you tell the story, I think I know why he was scared. You came too close to uncovering the truth. He doesn't want to lose the money and power. I honestly don't think he feels guilty about anything he's done. It's kind of like all is fair in love and war. He just doesn't want to get caught and lose everything."

"What did he tell you when he called with the plans?" I ask. "Did he give you any indication as to where my daughter could be."

"He didn't say," Kevin tells me. "He just gave me the timeline and told me what my part of the plan would be. That's it."

"Well, do you have any idea where they could be? The police have checked out and searched every piece of property your grandfather and the judge own. We haven't come up with anything. You must have some clue where they could be," I say, trying not to sound desperate, although that's exactly what I am. But I'm trying to stay calm and let Kevin tell this his own way and in his own time. I don't want him to get angry and not tell me everything he knows or feels. What would be worse yet is if he got angrier enough to lie or send us on a wild goose chase.

"There might be one place," Kevin says.

My heart starts racing. Could this be it? Could this be the final step to finding Kathryn and Gina?

"Our families ... the Valentines and the Vaughns ... own a couple acres of property near Seneca Rocks. It's in my father's name. Tax purposes or something. That's why you wouldn't know they own it. But that could be where they are. It's out of the way. No traffic. No one would ever stumble upon them there."

"Can you give us directions?" I ask.

Kevin gives directions to the state trooper who will be leading the way on the hour-long trip from the barracks to the Vaughn and Valentine property. Kevin will be in that car. Richie and I will follow in another state police car.

This is sure to be one of the longest hours of my life.

Richie and I don't say a word during the drive. There really isn't anything to say anymore. All we can do is wait, and hope we're not too late.

During the drive, I'm thinking about Kathryn almost constantly. It seems I'm remembering every minute, every second of her life. I remember how overjoyed I was when she was born. Of course I wanted a boy, but I couldn't be happier with my daughter. She means the world to me and I don't know what I'd do without her.

When I'm not thinking about Kathryn, I'm thinking about Gina. I wonder if she would have been so deeply involved in this mess if she and I hadn't started our friendship. It's because of this mess that we have a relationship at all other than work, but still I have to wonder. Beyond that, I wonder if she'll end up resenting me for getting her this involved. She's a grown woman and capable of making her own choices, but would she have made the choice to get this involved in the story if not for me?

A bigger question is: If she doesn't resent me, where do we go from here? I thought I'd never want another woman in my life after Vanessa. But now, although we've only been together - if you can call it that - for a very short time, I can't imagine my life without Gina.

There are too many questions and not enough answers. The biggest question, aside from where are Kathryn and Gina, is: Who killed Danny Dwyer? We still don't know. We know who was behind it. We have the motive. But we don't know who pulled the trigger. Will we ever?

# Chapter Thirty-seven

At the end of a long, winding driveway that goes up a hill, the police car in front of us stops. Kevin is escorted out of the car and into the unmarked police car that was following Richie and me. Earlier, we had decided it would be best if Kevin drove up to the house himself to check out the situation. He's wired so we'll be able to hear everything as we wait at the bottom of the hill.

We watch as Kevin drives up the hill. We wait for what seems like hours, but is actually only a couple of minutes, as Kevin gets out of the car and walks to the front door. He knocks, then walks inside and calls for his grandfather.

At first we don't hear anything, then we hear a voice in the background getting closer and closer.

"What the hell are you doing here?" Bill Valentine asks Kevin.

"I think the police are onto you, Granddad," Kevin says. I'm surprised that Kevin has the piece of mind to call Valentine "Granddad," thus positively identifying him for us. As if I wouldn't be able to recognize the voice that's tormented me for years.

"What makes you say that?" Valentine asks.

"I have a gut feeling," Kevin says. "I think you need to get that little girl and that reporter out of here, then disappear."

"How do you know the girl and the reporter are here?" Valentine asks.

"Another gut feeling," Kevin says. "Are they here?"

"Yes they're here," Valentine says. "Where else would we take them? We'll let them go as soon as we figure out what we're going to do and where we're going to go."

Thank God, I think to myself. We found them. Finally! Now, to get to them.

"Where are you going to go?" Kevin asks. "What are you talking about?"

"Obviously we can't go back to Brafferd County," Valentine says. "We can't even stay in the country. We're figuring out the fastest, easiest way to liquidate our assets and get out of here. It's past time for us to retire anyway. We're just going to do it sooner than we expected and in a different country than we expected. It's a simple change of plans. That's all."

"If that's what you're doing," Kevin says, "why the kidnapping? Why go to all that trouble?"

Someone briefed Kevin quite well on what to ask his grandfather, I think to myself. I hate to say this, but he's doing a great job. Let's hope he keeps it up and doesn't blow it before we get to Kathryn and Gina.

As Kevin grills his grandfather, the backup police officers and state troopers that were called in surround the grounds and the house. Now that we know Kathryn and Gina are here, we just have to wait for the right moment to move in and get them.

"We went to all that trouble, as you call it," Valentine says, "to throw everyone off the track."

"Off what track?" Kevin asks.

"Danny Dwyer, you idiot," Valentine says. "If the police and Joe Manzarelli are concentrating on the kidnapping, they can't dig any deeper into Dwyer's death. With Gina Hamilton out of the picture, she can't do any more damage either. By the time we let her go and she writes an article about all of this, Warren and I will be comfortably lounging on a beach somewhere."

"You think this is going to make everyone forget about Danny Dwyer?" Kevin asks. "You don't think they've already started digging deeper?"

"You know," Valentine says, "you're acting pretty high and mighty all of a sudden. If you'd taken care of all of this in the first place like we told you to back then, none of this would be happening now."

"You're blaming me now?" Kevin asks.

"You're the one who couldn't follow simple instructions," Valentine says.

"Simple instructions?" Kevin says. "You wanted me to give Danny a lethal injection. No matter what anyone thinks, I liked Danny Dwyer. We were friends and you told me you wanted me to kill him."

"There you go rationalizing again," Valentine says. "You didn't seem to have a problem watching him die slowly, watching his mind and body deteriorate with all the drugs you fed him with. But when I tell you to get it over with quickly, all of a sudden you have morals."

"Doing what you wanted me to do would have been murder, Granddad. I couldn't do that."

"And that's why you're only a business manager at one of the dealerships," Valentine says. "If you knew how to follow instructions, you'd have your own business by now, just like your cousins and Warren's nephews."

"The business is the last thing on my mind right now," Kevin says. "What I'm concerned with now is that you and Judge Vaughn finally do the right thing."

"And what, in your opinion, is the right thing?"

"Let Gina Hamilton and Kathryn Manzarelli go. Send them home. Now."

"You think it's that easy, do you?"

"Yes," Kevin says. "It's that easy."

"Well, my boy, I hate to burst your bubble, but it's not that easy."

"Why not? Just let them go before you lose your temper and ..."

"And what?"

"You know what I mean."

"No. Enlighten me."

"Before you lose your temper and kill them like you killed Danny."

It was Bill Valentine! Bill Valentine killed Danny Dwyer. He pulled the trigger. I should have known. Maybe I did know all along and brushed it off believing it was just wishful thinking to assume he could do something so heinous then cover it up.

"Who says I killed him?" Valentine says. "Did you see me pull the trigger?"

"No," Kevin says. "I just assumed ..."

"You assumed Warren wouldn't want to get his hands dirty," Valentine says. "Well, you're right. He agreed that we had to stop Danny Dwyer from talking, but he thought reasoning with him would do the trick. He was wrong. We tried for hours telling him how keeping quiet would be in everyone's best interests, but he wasn't buying it. He said he was going to the authorities and he was going to spill his guts.

"Warren is the one who lost his temper first. He even went as far as to go out to his car and get the gun. He thought threatening Danny with that would make him agree to keep quiet. But Danny was stubborn. He kept telling us to get out and saying we couldn't tell him what to do. He laughed whenever Warren waved the gun. He said neither of us had the guts to shoot a gun. He taunted us, making both of us angrier and angrier. Warren even had the gun pointed at Danny, but then changed his mind and started to walk away. I started to follow Warren, then Danny called us 'sick, cowardly bastards.' I grabbed the gun from Warren, turned around and gave Danny what he was asking for."

"So, you did pull the trigger," Kevin says.

"Yes, I pulled the trigger," Valentine says. "It wasn't long before you came back to the house. A few minutes later, Manzarelli showed up with blood on his hands and clothes from the fight he got into with you. Until we saw Manzarelli, we didn't know what we were going to do to cover up the shooting. We thought about saying it was accidental, but knew that wouldn't fly. We'd need to produce the gun and knew we couldn't explain why Judge Warren Vaughn's gun was at Danny Dwyer's apartment.

"Then Manzarelli arrived. We figured we'd point just enough fingers at him to raise suspicions and point everyone in the wrong direction, away from us. We told Chief Needham to rule the death a suicide to further confuse people. With a possible suspect and a little confusion added to the mix, we thought no one would ever get close enough to connect us to Danny Dwyer's death."

Richie's holding me back. If he wasn't, I'd be running up to the house and killing Bill Valentine with my bare hands. He put me through all those years of hell to cover up the fact that he killed my best friend. And for what? Money and power. Danny was right. Valentine is a sick bastard.

"We thought we were in the clear," Valentine continues. "For years, no one said anything about the Dwyers. Then that reporter had to open up the can of worms all over again. When she hooked up with Manzarelli, we knew that could be trouble. We tried scaring her by having Bud and Henry run her car off the road. We tried scaring Manzarelli by having Butch and Smitty hold his daughter overnight. But did that stop them? No. There was only one thing left to do before it was too late and they uncovered the truth. We had to throw them off the trail and scare them at the same time. That's why we planned the second kidnapping. We had to buy some time until we can get out of the country. When we're gone, we'll let everyone know where to find Gina Hamilton and Manzarelli's daughter."

"Are you going to keep them here until then?" Kevin asks.

"It's the best place for them," Valentine says. "It's out of the way. No one's likely to stumble upon them by accident. Before we leave, we'll cut the phone lines so they won't be able to call anyone who would be smart enough to look at airports for us. After we reach our destination, we'll send word that they're here. When the police find them, they'll discover that the two of them have been living quite comfortably with everything they could possibly need."

"I'm glad to hear you've got it all worked out," Kevin says. I wonder if Valentine notices the sarcasm dripping from Kevin's voice. "Where are the judge, Gina and Kathryn right now?"

"In the kitchen having a snack," Valentine says. "See? I told you they'd be comfortable and we'd take good care of them. Would you like to join us for a snack."

As Kevin follows his grandfather into the kitchen, the police move in. All they were waiting for was a specific location in the house. The faster they can get to Kathryn and Gina once they're inside, the less likely it would be that they'd be hurt in the rescue attempt.

All we hear over the microphone hooked up to the hardware Kevin's wearing is noise and static. We can't tell what's happening.

It sounds chaotic and I'm chomping at the bit. I need to get up to the house. I need to see Kathryn and Gina and know that they're safe and unharmed. But Richie keeps holding me back. He tells me we can't go up to the house until the men up there give us the okay.

I know I've mentioned this time and time again, but I'm not good at waiting. This is driving me crazy. Kathryn and Gina are so close and I can't get to them yet. What's taking so long? Richie tells me it's only been three minutes since the police got into the house. Give it time, he tells me. But I've been giving it time. I need to see my daughter. Now.

Although Richie tells me only three more minutes have passed, it seems like an hour before we get a call on the police radio.

"All clear," the officer says. "Mr. Manzarelli, there are two young ladies here who I think will be very happy to see you."

# Chapter Thirty-eight

It's hard to believe two weeks have passed since I brought Kathryn and Gina home. Sometimes it seems like only yesterday. Other times it seems as if nothing bad ever happened and we've been living like this forever.

But bad things did happen, and the people that made them happen will be spending years in prison, exactly where they belong.

Gina took great pleasure in seeing that the articles concerning this mess made the front page of the paper for a week. Of course, because of her involvement, she didn't get a byline on any of them. After each article, in italics, was the sentence "Century reporter Gina Hamilton contributed to this story."

Did she ever.

She's decided, however, that she's not quite ready to leave *The Century*. She wants to keep working there a little longer and save some money to live on while she's writing her award-winning screenplay.

As long as she's happy. I'm happy. Personally, I think working at *The Century* stresses her out too much. But, if there's one thing I've learned about Gina it's not to try to change her mind when it's set on something. So, my greatest contribution, I think, is helping her relieve her stress when she gets home.

The custody hearing is still two weeks away, but Kathryn's been spending most of her time with me. I'd hate to think the impossible happened and Vanessa realized she's not a good mother after all, but I can't think of any other explanation. Knowing Vanessa the way I do, though, I'm sure that once she gets back from Aruba she'll be ready to fight. But I'm not nervous. I'm very confident that I'll get full custody of Kathryn.

With Kathryn here, and Gina here most of the time, it feels like a family.

I haven't mentioned the word love to Gina yet, but I'm pretty sure I'm there. I have a feeling she is, too. But, as serious as we seem to be getting, we made a pact. We're not going to sleep together while Kathryn's home. As much as Kathryn loves Gina, we're not quite sure how she'd feel about us having an intimate relationship. And, in no way, am I ready to talk to my daughter about that.

Other than that, all is well. Right now, Kathryn's getting ready for bed and Gina's taking a bubble bath. Kathryn talked her into it by saying it was a good stress reliever. I'll never get used to eight-year-olds knowing about stress and how to relieve it. Anyway, I'm here in the kitchen smiling while I pour a glass of wine for Gina. If the bubble bath doesn't relax her, the wine should.

I walk slowly into the steamy bathroom because Gina's eyes are closed and, at first, I think she might be asleep and I don't want to disturb her. I place the wineglass on the floor next to her and try to sneak out.

"Where are you going?" she asks, with her eyes still closed.

"I didn't want to disturb you."

"You never disturb me," she says, opening her eyes. "Come over here."

I walk back over to the bathtub.

"Now, kiss me," she says.

"If I must," I tease.

She reaches up, grabs my shirt and pulls me down to her. We kiss. And kiss. She pulls me closer. I sit on the edge of the tub, dip my hand in the water then run my hand up and down her leg.

She pulls me closer to her as our kiss becomes more passionate.

"Daddy!" we hear Kathryn yell from the bedroom. Gina and I pull away from each other. "I forgot I'm supposed to bring cupcakes to school tomorrow."

Gina and I look at each other not quite sure whether to laugh or, well, I don't know what.

"I'll be there in a minute, Kitty Kat," I yell back to her.

"I guess that's what we get for getting that close to breaking our pact," Gina says. "This is gonna be hard."

"Very hard," I say.

I kiss Gina one more time, then go to find out what kind of cupcakes I'll be baking.